ABOUT THE AUTHOR

Michael Coleman was born in Forest Gate,
East London. In his life journey from aspiring
footballer to full-time writer he has variously been
employed as a waiter, a computer programmer,
a university lecturer, a software quality assurance
consultant and a charity worker. He is married,
with four children and one grandchild.

Michael has written many novels, including the
Carnegie Medal shortlisted *Weirdo's War*. His website
can be found at www.michael-coleman.com

The Fighting Pit is the second gripping title in
The Bear Kingdom trilogy. Look out for the first
book, *The Howling Tower*, and the final
instalment – *The Hunting Forest*.

Acclaim for *Weirdo's War*:

'Tense, psychological and instructive.' *The Times*

As thought-provoking as it is exciting...addresses
fundamental truths about human character
and behaviour.' *Booktrusted News*

For Barry and Brenda

ORCHARD BOOKS
338 Euston Road, London NW1 3BH
Orchard Books Australia
Hachette Children's Books
Level 17, 207 Kent Street, Sydney, NSW 2000, Australia

ISBN-10: 1 84616 214 9
ISBN-13: 978 1 84616 214 5

First published in 2006 by Orchard Books
A paperback original
Text © Wordjuggling Limited 2006
The right of Michael Coleman to be identified as
the author of this work has been asserted by him in
accordance with the Copyright, Designs and Patents Act, 1988.
A CIP catalogue record for this book is available from the British Library.

1 3 5 7 9 10 8 6 4 2
Printed in Great Britain

Orchard Books is a division of Hachette Children's Books

THE BEAR KINGDOM

THE
FIGHTING
PIT

MICHAEL COLEMAN

ORCHARD BOOKS

CONTENTS

THE SAP-GARDEN

Benjamin Wildfire and Mops headed deep into Shadewell-Wood, rejoicing with every step that they were getting further and further away from the horrors of the Howling-Tower.

Even so, the thought of running into a bear – any bear – filled them with terror. So they travelled only at night, from sun-go until the first fingers of sun-come were feeling their way into the sky. During the light-time they kept well hidden. Dark and muddy cavities beneath the roots of fallen trees were especially useful, if not pleasant.

'Look at the *state* of my *dress*!' Mops had wailed more than once.

Her once-pretty pink outfit, which had become very dirty and bedraggled during their time caged in the Howling-Tower, was now in tatters. Shreds of material dangled down from the hem and embarrassing holes revealed the pink things she had on beneath.

'I don't suppose I look much better,' said Benjamin, finally.

Mops had looked him up and down. 'You're right. You don't.'

Although Benjamin's outfit had hardly any holes, it – along with his red hair – was now caked in mud. In his case this was actually a good thing, for the suit he was wearing had once been bright orange. It was the uniform of a Howling-Tower trusty-sap. In that accursed place a few humans had been trained to work. One of these, known to them only as Number Twelve, had bravely helped Benjamin escape by giving him his suit to wear.

Moving through Shadewell-Wood in darkness hadn't been easy. Parts were open and smooth but, in others, clutching branches and piercing thorns had slowed them to a crawl. Finally, early on the fourth night following their escape from the Howling-Tower, the wood began to thin. Through the trees they could see a torch-lit track, with a steady stream of carts trundling along it.

After a while the stream of carts slowed to a trickle. Still frightened about being spotted, Benjamin and Mops ventured only very slowly out from the cover of the wood. Dodging in and out of the shadows, they followed the curving line of the cart-track. It brought them to a sprawling group of dens.

Most of these dens were grey and mound-shaped, with stained slate roofs which sloped down almost to the ground. Their wide wooden doorways were dimly lit and gloomy. None showed any sign of being occupied. But on the edge of the sprawling group there was one, very much larger den, which looked quite different. It had dozens of twinkling torch-posts mounted along its front. What was more, it was most certainly occupied. From within, and also from a fenced-off section at its rear, they could hear the laughing growls and bellowing roars of bears having a rowdily good time. Benjamin and Mops crept closer.

'I can smell nut-doughs!' hissed Mops suddenly.

The mere mention of the word was enough to make Benjamin's mouth start watering. For a nut-dough – unlike other bear-foods, such as grated turnip or squashed hornet – tasted as delicious to a human as to a bear. It was made by mixing crushed beech nuts, hazel nuts and chestnuts into a soft sticky ball of dough, baking this ball over an open fire, then serving it piping hot and dripping with a layer of golden honey.

The smell also reminded Benjamin of just how hungry he was. As they'd made their way through Shadewell-Wood, he and Mops had been able to find sufficient wild fruits and nuts to keep from starving, but certainly not enough to fill them completely.

They crept closer. The opening to a dark and narrow cobbled alley lay just a few paces away. Benjamin tiptoed across and peered in.

'Where do you think it leads, Mops?' he whispered.

'I shudder to think,' replied Mops.

The alley was grimy and littered with rubbish. At the far end they could just make out a solitary torch-post. But before then, beyond where the pale walls of the noisy den ended, a glow of light was spilling into the alley from above a stretch of high wooden fencing.

And not only light. In spite of her shudders, Mops had ventured further into the alley. 'The nut-dough smell is definitely coming from down here,' she said, her nose twitching.

Without another word, she began to tip-toe along the rubbish-strewn cobbles to where the fence began. Benjamin followed, glancing anxiously over his shoulder to make sure that no bear was following *him*. By the time they reached the point where the stretch of fencing started, the smells had become even stronger. So too had the noise. From the other side of the fence, not only had the growls and roars grown louder, they'd grown fiercer. These were no longer the sounds of bears simply having a good time.

'What are they doing in there?' gasped Mops, as what sounded like a howl of torment rose above the roars.

Benjamin had no idea. Neither did he think it a good idea to stop and find out, enticing as the nut-dough smells were. The terrifying sounds coming from beyond the fence told him that the best thing they could do was leave – and quickly. So when, a short way ahead of him,

Mops stopped at a gap in the fence and looked as if she was thinking of diving through, he hissed, 'Keep going!'

'I can't!'

'You've got to! Forget the nut-doughs, Mops. It's too dangerous to stay around here!'

'And I'm telling you I can't keep going!' squeaked Mops. 'Because there's a bear ahead!'

As she shrank back against the fence, Benjamin saw what she'd seen. In the pool of light cast by the single torch-post at the far end of the alley was the unmistakeable silhouette of a large, upright bear. It was facing sideways, one curved claw beckoning to some unseen companion.

'Back the way we came, Mops!' hissed Benjamin.

He turned, ready to run – only to stop. Another frightening bear silhouette had appeared at that end of the alley too. This one was even more menacing, for it showed that this bear was wielding a thick, club-like weapon.

'We're trapped!' cried Mops. 'What are we going to do now?'

Unusually for Mops, it was a silly question. There was only one thing they could do.

With a deep breath they dived through the gap in the fence and into the sea of noise and smells on the other side...

They found themselves behind two huge acorn-wood

barrels, twice as tall as them and three times as wide. Benjamin and Mops were beautifully hidden (as was the hole in the broken fence, which explained why it hadn't been noticed and fixed before now). They risked a quick peep out and saw two long tubes snaking away from the barrels and across the grass. The end of one of the tubes had a slight leak in it, and a small puddle of liquid had formed on the ground near where they were crouching. It smelled truly awful.

'What is that stuff? hissed Mops, wrinkling her nose.

Benjamin knew. 'It's hops-drink.' He peered through the gap between the two barrels. 'And that must be a drinking-hole,' he pointed.

Mops took a look herself. The tube leading from the barrel ended at a hole in the ground. At least, she could only assume it was a hole. The edges weren't visible because the hole was overflowing with foam.

'You mean bears *swallow* that stuff? And *live*?'

Remembering the cruel owner he'd first escaped from, Benjamin nodded. 'Mrs Haggard, used to drink it sometimes. She'd come home smelling of it and tottering from side to side.' He pointed again. 'A bit like them!'

A couple of bears were waddling unsteadily towards the drinking-hole, laugh-growling as they went. A heavy, miserable-looking she-bear seemed to be guarding the hole. The two bears had to give her some payment before they were allowed to bury their snouts in the foam and begin slurping greedily.

'Up-time!' roared the hole-keeper after a little while.

Grumbling about being short-timed, the two drinkers lumbered off. The gap between the barrels wasn't wide enough for Benjamin and Mops to see where they went. They risked leaning around the side of one of the barrels. Not far, but far enough to see that they'd stumbled into a large, square, fenced-off area, thronged with noisy bears. And, in particular, to realise that they'd found out where the delicious nut-dough smells had been coming from.

The two drinker-bears had gone straight to where a short, sweating bear with a pair of tongs in his paw was standing beside a crackling fire. On a griddle laid across this fire were dozens of round balls of golden brown dough. The nut-dough seller finished serving a mean-looking bear holding a long stick. Then, in return for more money, he lifted two balls from the griddle, trickled honey over each, and handed them to the laugh-growling drinkers.

'What are these places?' hissed Mops. 'Did your Mrs Haggard ever say anything before she went out?'

(This question wasn't as odd as it might seem. It was well known that bears talked to their human pets constantly, even though they didn't believe for one moment that they were being understood).

'Yes, she did sometimes,' said Benjamin. 'She'd say, "Bum-fluff!" – that was one of the names she called me – "Off-me to the sap-garden!"'

'The *sap*-garden?' echoed Mops. 'Why call it that, when the place is only used by…'

She had been going to say 'bears'. And she would have done, had it not been for the terrible howl that suddenly came from the centre of the garden. For that howl – the same as they'd heard out in the alley – hadn't come from any bear. It could only have come, they now realised, from a sap: a human being. A human in torment.

Horrified by what they'd just heard, Benjamin and Mops risked leaning out even further from their hiding place. In the very centre of the garden a group of bears were gathered in a circle. They were grunting and hooting fiercely. Suddenly, as that same awful howl rose again, the circle parted to show what was happening.

The mean-looking bear they'd seen being served with a nut-dough had stuck it onto the end of his long stick. He was now in the very centre of the bear circle. With him was a howling human.

The human was perhaps six or seven summers older than Benjamin, and strong, but it was clear he hadn't been fed for a good while. With his eyes fixed on the nut-dough as if it was the only thing in Bear Kingdom, he was leaping as high as he could to try and reach it.

'Jump, Roger Broadback!' the stick-holding bear was hollering.

But every time poor Roger Broadback jumped the stick was twitched out of reach, causing him to howl in anguish yet again.

'He's tiring,' said Benjamin.

In the centre of the bear circle Roger Broadback was now gasping for breath. He was still desperately trying to get hold of the nut-dough, but all the spring had gone out of his weary legs. The bear held his stick temptingly lower. With one final attempt Roger leapt – only for his fingers to fall tantalisingly short, as the tormenting bear knew they would. To a loud roar from those in the circle Roger Broadback collapsed in a heap, moaning pitifully.

Another bear stepped into the circle. He had a board on which the number 436 had been scratched. He held this aloft as he marched around the circle shouting, 'Roger Broadback, owner Ursus Covet, count-lasted four-three-six! Four-three-six! Bet-settle now!'

'That's disgraceful!' hissed Mops. 'They were trying to win money by guessing how long that poor Roger Broadback would keep on jumping before he collapsed!'

Around the circle, clinking coins were changing paws. None of them had come the way of Ursus Covet, though. Having roughly dragged the exhausted Roger Broadback to his feet, the angry bear was now hauling him across to the nearby fence.

'Lost-you-me money-good,' Benjamin and Mops heard him snarl. 'Bet-me count-you-last five-hundred!'

Not far from their hiding place a strong length of rope hung from a hook embedded in a fence post. On reaching it, Ursus Covet looped this rope around Roger

Broadback's waist and tied his hands behind his back. Then, as if wanting to be as cruel as he possibly could, the mean bear leaned the stick with its fragrant nut-dough right beside him.

With that, Ursus Covet turned back to the circle of bears. A loud burst of laugh-cheers had told him that the next event was about to begin. On the far side of the sap-garden, Benjamin saw another starving and wretched young human had been untied by his owner and was being thrust towards the waiting circle.

'Look, Mops,' hissed Benjamin, 'there are more!' He pointed towards the other humans he'd only just noticed, all tied to different parts of the sap-garden fence. 'Two over there, one in the corner, one right down at the end... Is that what a sap-garden really is, a place where humans are tormented just for fun?'

No answer.

'Mops?' He swung round. 'Mops! What are you doing?'

Mops hadn't answered his question for the simple reason that she hadn't heard it. She'd been crawling out from their hiding place on her hands and knees. As to what she was doing, Benjamin could see only too well. She was heading for the tied-up Roger Broadback. Or was she?

Mops had stopped at the long stick leaning against the fence. Still crouching on the ground, she now took hold of the end of the stick – and began moving it, not

16

away from Roger Broadback as the tormenting Ursus Covet had done, but towards his mouth. The starving Roger, unable to believe his eyes as the nut-dough finally came his way, bit into it with a loud cry of joy: a cry so loud and joyful that it could be heard above the excited babble of the circle of bears.

And heard it was, by Ursus Covet. Swinging round from his place on the edge of the circle, Roger Broadback's owner was just in time to see his sap gulping down the nut-dough…and, still with the stick in her hands, the girl-sap who'd given it to him. With an angry roar, Ursus Covet began to lumber in Mops's direction.

Benjamin didn't hesitate. Leaping out from behind the barrels he raced over and grabbed Mops by the hand. 'Run!' he screeched.

In his panic, Benjamin completely forgot about the gap in the fence through which they'd got into the sap-garden. Instead, he began to drag Mops towards the far end, hoping to find a way out there. They didn't reach it. The bears in the circle, their attention attracted by Ursus Covet's roar of rage, showed how quickly large bears can move if they need to. As Benjamin and Mops ran towards them, they quickly strung themselves out right across their path. All the two friends could do was skid to one side to avoid them.

But all that had done was send them running into the very centre of the garden. The moment they did so the bear circle began to form again. They quickly found a solid wall of bears blocking the way ahead. They spun round...and round...and round...and stopped.

There was no longer any place for them to run to. The bears had completed their circle once more – and Benjamin and Mops were in the middle of it.

CHANCELLOR BRUNO

'Bet-time, thinks-me,' said a deep and menacing voice.

It belonged to Ursus Covet. The circle had parted briefly to allow him through, then closed up again. Roger Broadback's owner had a cold smile on his face. His long stick was back between his claws – but this time Ursus Covet hadn't speared a nut-dough on its end.

'If saps-these stick-whipped,' he said to the laugh-growling audience, 'bets-who last-them count-thirty before blood-dripping…?'

Terrified, Benjamin and Mops clutched each other tightly – especially when Ursus Covet added chillingly, '…Or fifty-over before blood-pouring?'

From around the circle eager paws held up coins to place their bets. In no time at all, the deals were done. Ursus Covet turned back to Benjamin and Mops. He looked from one to the other, swishing the stick viciously to and fro.

'Now, first-who?' he said to himself.

'Neither of us!' shrieked Mops. 'Why can't you just leave us alone? What have we done to hurt you?'

Benjamin didn't bother wasting words when he knew the bears couldn't understand them. He just stepped silently in front of Mops so that Ursus Covet would reach him first.

A ripple of excitement swept round the circle. Eyes glinted in anticipation. Lips were licked at the thought of what was to come. A chant began, growing louder: 'Sap-thrash! Sap-thrash!'

Ursus Covet drew himself up onto his hind legs so that he was towering over the trembling Benjamin. Squeezing his eyes tightly shut, Benjamin braced himself for the first, agonising blow...

It didn't come.

For, even as Roger Broadback's owner raised his stick high into the air, the chanting of the bear-circle was silenced by a bellow filled with authority:

'Stop-you in name-the of King Antonius!'

And bursting into the sap-garden from all directions came the bears that Benjamin and Mops had first seen gathering outside in the alleyway.

Benjamin flicked open his eyes. 'What's going on, Mops?' he hissed.

'I don't know,' Mops whispered back, 'but it looks serious, whatever it is.'

The circle surrounding them had already broken up, with most of the bears shuffling nervously towards the sap-garden's fences. Even the thunder-faced Ursus Covet had lowered his stick and taken a step backwards.

Whatever this squad's business was, Roger Broadback's owner clearly had no more intention of standing in their way than any of the others.

'Forward-step owners-all of saps-these!' barked the voice of authority.

This time Benjamin and Mops saw who this voice belonged to. As they slid slowly away from Ursus Covet and towards the shadows, a powerful black bear with a vivid claw-scar running from one eye down to his snout stalked into the centre of the garden. Like every member of the squad he commanded, he was armed with a bear's favourite weapon: a short, thick, very hard wooden club known as a cruncheon. As he'd asked his question, the scar-faced bear had been moving this cruncheon slowly in an arc. Now, as it stopped, that cruncheon was pointing straight at the tied-up figure of Roger Broadback.

'Him! Who him-owns?'

Ursus Covet took a hesitant step forward. Gone was his bullying manner. He had a big, oily smile across his face. 'Mine-he-is, Chancellor Bruno,' Ursus Covet simpered. 'Name-his-be Roger Broadback. Though times-some names-me-use nice-so-not,' he added with a sickly laugh-growl.

Chancellor Bruno showed not a flicker of amusement at this joke. He began to count out coins from a bulging pouch hanging from a chain round his waist.

'Bought-he-is by King Antonius, for rounds-twenty.'

'But…but…' spluttered Ursus Covet, 'not-me-want him-sell!'

Chancellor Bruno simply shrugged. 'When King Antonius buy-wants, you sell-want.'

'But – for rounds-twenty?' Ursus Covet wrung his paws in anguish. 'Roger Broadback worth-is more-much!'

'Not-can King Antonius more-afford.'

The prospect of losing his sap was making Ursus Covet foolhardy. 'Pah!' he snorted. 'The king rich-is! The king afford-can price-any!'

Moments later he was regretting his outburst. At the merest of nods from Chancellor Bruno, two of his squad leapt forward. Beating Ursus Covet about the back and head with their heavy cruncheons, they drove him, howling, from the sap-garden.

'For galley-saps, pays King Antonius rounds-twenty and more-no!' snapped Chancellor Bruno. He gazed bleakly at the silent bears who obviously owned the other humans tied to the sap-garden's fence. 'But less-much to argue-owners.'

If any of the other owners had been thinking of arguing, the treatment handed out to Ursus Covet had changed their minds. Each meekly stepped up to accept their twenty rounds in payment, then left the sap-garden.

All this time, Benjamin and Mops had been retreating unnoticed into the shadows. They'd then begun inching towards the shelter of the two huge barrels behind which they'd first hidden. They'd got to within five paces of the tied-up Roger Broadback but when Benjamin heard Ursus Covet's claim that King Antonius was rich enough to afford any price for a sap he'd stopped dead.

'Mops! Did you hear what he said?' he gasped, his heart pounding. 'The King of the Bears is rich. It could have been him who bought my mother!'

For that's exactly what he'd been told by Twelve, the trusty-sap who'd helped them escape from the Howling-Tower: that after his father, Duncan, had himself escaped from that evil place, his mother, Alicia, had been bought by an unknown bear who could afford any price.

'Oh, Benjamin!' gasped Mops. 'You could be right!'

Out in the centre of the sap-garden, Chancellor Bruno had begun to supervise the next stage of his operation. Having completed his sap purchases, he wanted them brought together for inspection. Two thick-browed, cruncheon-wielding members of his squad were heading straight for Roger Broadback.

'Stay out of sight, both of you!' he hissed at Benjamin and Mops, 'unless you want to become galley-saps as well!'

Moments later, with Benjamin and Mops crouching nearby in the shadows, the two squad-bears were untying Roger Broadback and feeling his spindly, undernourished arms.

'Huh! Little-use one-this till up-him-fattened!' said the first.

The other laugh-grunted in agreement. 'Seen-me sticks-thicker than arms-these!'

'Still, hear-me sap-food good-is on the Galley-Royal of King Antonius and Queen Dearie!' growled the first with what sounded like jealousy. 'Better than bear-food.'

'The Galley-Royal?' hissed Benjamin as Roger Broadback was led away into the centre of the garden to be roped together with the other saps. 'Where in Bear Kingdom is that?'

'A place where they need galley-saps, I suppose,' answered Mops. 'And lots of them.'

'What for, though? What do galley-saps do?'

'Whatever the king and queen want them to do,' said Mops. Her voice took on a dreamy, faraway sound. 'In return for food. Lovely food. Better than bear-food food…'

But Benjamin's mind was on other matters. 'Mops, if the king is rich enough to afford anything… and he did buy my mother…then it could be that she – she…' His voice cracked with emotion.

Mops finished the sentence for him. 'Ended up as a galley-sap, whatever that is, and is living in the king and queen's Galley-Royal, wherever *that* is.'

Benjamin nodded tearfully.

Mops sighed. 'Well, we won't find out the answers

to anything skulking around here in the shadows, will we?'

And with that she strode boldly out towards the scarred face and menacing cruncheon of the astonished Chancellor Bruno.

THE GALLEY-ROYAL

'What this-is?' Benjamin heard Chancellor Bruno growl as Mops strode boldly into the light. 'A sap-stray?'

He followed uncertainly, to hear the bear correct himself and say, '*Two* sap-strays?'

Benjamin gulped with fear. He hadn't the slightest idea what Mops was up to. Yes, he'd been hoping they might think of some way of reaching the mysterious Galley-Royal – but not like this, giving themselves up to Chancellor Bruno!

It was only as Mops reached the scar-faced bear that Benjamin realised that her plan was cleverer than that. Nose in the air, Mops hardly gave the chancellor a look. Instead, she marched straight past him to where an anxious Roger Broadback was now roped together in a line with the other humans bought for the king.

'We're with him!' announced Mops loudly – and, to make sure Chancellor Bruno got the message (because he hadn't understood what she'd said, of course) she promptly clamped herself to Roger Broadback's side like a limpet. More through trust than understanding, Benjamin quickly did the same and attached himself to Roger's other side.

'What in Bear Kingdom are you two doing?' hissed Roger Broadback.

'We're coming with you,' said Mops brightly. 'To the Galley-Royal.'

'To be a galley-sap,' said Benjamin, trying to sound just as confident as Mops.

'Are you mad?' cried Roger Broadback.

'QUIET-BE!' roared Chancellor Bruno.

Shocked into silence, Mops edged behind Roger Broadback's gangly legs. From the other side, Benjamin did very much the same. But at a sign from Chancellor Bruno a couple of cruncheon-wielding bears scurried forward and dragged them out into the open.

The scar-faced bear looked down at Benjamin and Mops. 'Sap-strays or with-this Roger-sap,' he grunted, 'good-them-no for galley-saps!'

Behind him, Benjamin heard Roger Broadback murmur strangely, 'Think yourselves lucky.' *What exactly was a galley-sap?* he wondered.

'On paw-other,' Chancellor Bruno went on, 'free-they-come. And Queen Dearie bargain-likes.'

One of the bears who'd tested Roger Broadback's arms gave a polite snuffle-cough. 'If-likes Queen Dearie, Sir, then always-likes King Antonius.'

A look of contempt crossed Chancellor Bruno's

27

face. 'True-is-that!' he snorted. 'The king-she-has round-wrapped her claw-little.'

The large bear scratched his chin thoughtfully. Finally, he came to a decision. With a gesture, he had Benjamin and Mops roped to either side of Roger Broadback. 'Will-say found-me offer-special,' he laughed crudely, 'one-buy, free-two!'

With Benjamin, Mops and Roger at its head, the straggling line of humans was led out of the sap-garden to the cart-way that Benjamin and Mops had followed earlier. But they didn't turn in the direction of Shadewell-Wood. Instead, they turned the opposite way, towards a bright glow in the distance.

Chancellor Bruno marched arrogantly in front. The cart-way was now busy. Bears padded this way and that. Without exception, though, every single one of them – even the biggest and toughest – shrank back to let the line past the moment they saw who was leading it.

'Looks like he's important,' hissed Benjamin.

'Those in charge of money usually are,' replied Mops. 'Well, let's hope he's in charge of some brains as well. Enough to insist that when we get to this Galley-Royal place I'm allocated a task suited to my particular talents.'

'Such as?'

'Something light and in close proximity to food. A job like Queen Dearie's sap-in-waiting would do nicely. I used to fetch my previous owner's meals with a style that defied description.'

'You *are* mad,' muttered Roger Broadback between them. 'Both of you. But then I knew that. Only a mad girl would have taken the chance of getting that nut-dough for me. And only a mad boy would have joined her.' Roger smiled a gap-toothed smile. 'I thank you both heartily. I hope I will be able to repay you both some day – though I doubt it, where I'm going...'

Mops looked across at Benjamin. 'Who does he remind you of?' she sighed. 'Eh? Tell me.'

'Not – Spike?'

'Who else?' Mops looked up at Roger Broadback. 'An old friend of ours – well, of Benjamin's. Called everybody "matey" for some unfathomable reason. More to the point, he was a complete misery. It never occurred to him for one instant to look on the bright side. And...to be honest...you do seem a touch that way inclined yourself.'

'I'll try to remember that,' said Roger Broadback solemnly.

The mention of their friend Spike brought memories flooding back to Benjamin. Spike had escaped from the Howling-Tower at the same time as Mops, but when she'd insisted on waiting behind for Benjamin, Spike had left her and gone off on his own.

'Are you *sure* Spike didn't say where he was planning to go?' Benjamin asked for the umpteenth time.

'No!' said Mops irritably. 'His last words to me were, "I came here on my own and now I'm going on my own."' She sighed. 'No, I tell a lie. That's what he said before his last words. His actual last words to me were, "Goodbye – dearest Mops."'

'*Dearest*?' Benjamin smiled. 'I'm glad you two parted as friends.'

'Yes, well, I wouldn't go as far as to say that – but I don't deny I'm missing him.'

'Really?'

'Of course. Who do I have to complain about now?'

'Me?' grinned Benjamin.

'Oh, I can't make do with just you,' said Mops. 'A girl needs variety!'

They'd now been shuffling along for a fair while. They'd passed numerous dimly-lit caverns packed with bears and smelling of strange drinks. They'd passed trade-caverns offering goods of every description: from thick vine-ropes to weather-bad all-overs, from snout-grease to claw-sharpeners. And all the while a dank and filthy stench had been growing stronger.

'What is that disgusting smell?' asked Mops finally.

'What do you think it is?' answered Roger Broadback. 'The Winding-River.'

'Is that where we're going?' said Benjamin. 'Is that where the Galley-Royal is, beside the Winding-River?'

'Beside it? The Galley-Royal is *on* it.' Roger Broadback looked down at Benjamin and Mops and shook his head. 'You two don't know what the Galley-Royal is, do you?'

'Not…precisely,' said Mops. 'Why don't you fill us in on the details?'

'That won't take long,' said Roger. 'The Galley-Royal is the king and queen's personal galley-float. They use it to travel up and down the Winding-River between here and Bearkingdom-Palace.'

An awful realisation had begun to dawn on Benjamin. Hesitantly he asked, 'How does it move?'

'How do you think!' cried Roger Broadback. 'It's rowed along – by galley-saps! That's how I'm going to be spending the rest of my days, heaving on a rowing-pole until I'm not strong enough to do it any longer.'

As sorry as Benjamin felt for Roger's plight, he couldn't help feeling a sense of relief and excitement for himself. Chancellor Bruno had said that both he and Mops wouldn't be any use as galley-saps. That was a relief. But far more importantly, what he'd just heard filled him with excitement. Bearkingdom-Palace sounded a much more likely place for his mother, Alicia, to have been taken if she really had been bought by King Antonius. And, if Roger Broadback was right, the Galley-Royal might take him there! If Roger Broadback was right…

These thoughts were pushed to the back of Benjamin's mind as they suddenly turned a corner and came to a halt before a towering set of guarded gates. At a curt wave from Chancellor Bruno's cruncheon the gates immediately swung open. Through them they filed, onto a long, wide stretch of cobbled ground.

'The Quay-Royal,' whispered Mops, pointing at an ornate sign mounted on a post.

Roger Broadback gaped down at her. 'You can read?'

'Of course,' said Mops airily. 'I'm not just a pretty face, you know.'

Even without Mops's special talent Benjamin might have been able to work out what the Quay-Royal was: a place for boarding the Galley-Royal. For beyond the cobbled ground, looking a lot prettier than it smelled, the waters of the Winding-River were twinkling in the moonlight. Bobbing up and down on them was the Galley-Royal itself.

Its intricately claw-carved dark brown wood was inlaid with jewels. Gaily-coloured pennants fluttered above its decks. The royal standard hung grandly from its rear. Its prow carried the figure of a glamorous, but gaudily decorated, she-bear. A peppering of delicate torch-lights bathed the whole galley-float in a golden glow.

'Oh, how romantic!' sighed Mops.

Benjamin said nothing. If what Roger Broadback had said was true, they were going to find that inside the Galley-Royal was anything but romantic.

A wooden ramp led from the quay up to a gap high in the Galley-Royal's side. At the foot of this ramp a proud and perfectly-groomed grey bear was waiting.

Like most of the bears who'd stormed into the sap-garden with Chancellor Bruno, he had a shiny gold hoop dangling from the tip of his right ear.

'Ooh, I just *love* that ear-bling!' purred Mops.

As they reached the foot of the ramp, the waiting bear gave Chancellor Bruno a courteous bow.

'Successful out-night, Chancellor?' he asked in a gruff voice.

'See-yourself-that, Galley-Master,' smiled Chancellor Bruno.

The galley-master began prowling slowly up and down the line, starting and ending with Roger Broadback. An enormous chain full of keys, worn like a sash over his left shoulder, rattled as he moved.

'See-me galley-saps-eight,' said the galley-master, stroking his cheek with a carefully-clipped claw, 'rather *rib-skinny* galley-saps…'

'So up-them-fatten,' replied Chancellor Bruno.

The galley-master didn't respond. His attention was now wholly directed at Benjamin and Mops. 'But use-what these-are?'

'They nothing-cost,' shrugged Chancellor Bruno.

'And worth-them round-every,' growled the Galley-Master, unimpressed. 'Well-as-might them-throw river-in!'

At this threat Benjamin's heart began to thump alarmingly. His friend Spike had been a good swimmer but Benjamin had never tried and he suspected that it was a skill that took some learning. And even if he *could* swim, the stinky Winding-River — with the blobs of rotting vegetation and bear-ploppings floating on its surface — wasn't the place to try it. Frantically, Benjamin wriggled the wrist which was roped to Roger Broadback's. If only he could loosen it enough to slip his hand out…

What stopped him was Chancellor Bruno snorting, 'Them-throw river-in, Galley-Master? Ideal trap-rats?'

'Trap-rats?' The galley-master studied Benjamin and Mops more thoughtfully. 'Hmm. Be-could. Never-has the Galley-Royal enough trap-rats.' Moments later he'd come to a decision. 'Well-very! Aboard-them-take!'

They were pushed up the steep ramp to where a galley-bear was waiting for them. Extending two specially-sharpened claws, the galley-bear sliced neatly through the ropes connecting Benjamin and Mops to Roger Broadback and pushed them to one side.

'Goodbye,' was all Roger had time to say to them before being roughly led away to the front of the galley-float. There he disappeared from view down a flight of wooden steps.

One by one, the same thing happened to each of the other humans Chancellor Bruno had bought. After having their ropes cut, each was led off to descend the same set of steps.

'Looks like we're going somewhere else,' murmured Benjamin.

'*Every*where,' replied Mops, cheerfully. 'I think we are going to have the run of this place!'

'How? Why?'

'Simple,' said Mops. 'You heard them. We're going to be trap-rats. Now I can't say that particularly appeals – nasty little creatures rats, far too many teeth. I'll leave you to do the trapping part Benjamin – but the point is that we won't be able to trap rats if we're confined to one spot, will we? They'll have to let us move about.'

'So we might be able to find out more about the Galley-Royal?' said Benjamin.

'Like where the food is kept,' said Mops.

'And maybe even where my mother is,' said Benjamin hopefully.

'Precisely,' said Mops. 'Now, it only remains to be seen where they'll put us. Somewhere dry and comfortable, I trust.'

And so it was that, when the galley-master climbed the ramp and gave the order for Benjamin and Mops to be below-taken and made rat-ready, they weren't terribly worried.

Even when they were led, not down a set of steps, but to an open hatch in the middle of the Galley-Royal's rear deck, they thought little of it. It was only as they peered down through the hatch and into the black hole below that Mops gave a little squeak of uneasiness.

'That does not look comfortable,' she murmured.

A beam from an overhead torch-lantern illuminated the pools of water at the bottom of the hole. 'It's not dry, either,' said Benjamin.

Things then happened very quickly. Grabbed by a couple of rugged, ear-blinged galley-bears, both Benjamin and Mops had long lengths of rope tied round their waists. A third ear-blinged galley-bear (named Briny) then arrived carrying a pot of a liquid and a brush. The liquid didn't have any smell but it *was* very sticky – as Benjamin and Mops discovered when, with bold strokes, Briny sloshed a thick coat of the stuff over their bare arms and legs.

'Trap-rats ready-all, Galley-Master!' shouted Briny when he'd finished. 'Both-them-covered in poison-rat!'

'Rat poison?' gasped Mops. 'Oh, how could I have been so stupid? They don't want us to trap rats at all!'

'We *are* the rat traps!' cried Benjamin.

The galley-master loped forward, his keys jangling. 'Down-them-send!' he ordered.

Benjamin and Mops shouted and struggled, of course, but it was no use. With a galley-bear at the end of each rope, they were pushed through the hatch and lowered slowly down into the dark, wet hole.

36

TRAP-RATS

Benjamin and Mops sploshed down into a couple of filthy puddles. Above them they heard the galley-master warn his galley-bears, 'Ignore-you their scream-louds. Last-them long-not.'

They heard the hatch slam shut. It sounded heavy, and it was, but as he looked up Benjamin saw that the hatch wasn't a solid lump but a square grid of wooden beams. He could see out through the gaps.

'At least we can see the sky, Mops,' he said.

'Benjamin!' said Mops sharply, 'just for once will you please *not* try to look on the bright side! If that misery Spike was in here with us he'd be moaning that we're stuck in a wet and grubby hole waiting to be gnawed to the bone by an army of rats – and for once I'd be agreeing with him!'

'I'm not looking on the bright side,' said Benjamin thoughtfully. 'But I'm thinking that if light can get down here then it means we might be able to see enough to spot the rats before they get near us.'

'Oh. That's true.'

'Or,' added Benjamin, 'we might be able to see enough to find a place they can't reach.'

The hold-cargo (for that was the hole's correct name) was about half full. They'd been lowered into an open space in the centre. Around them, crates and bales were stacked halfway up to the roof. Exotic food smells were wafting from them, suggesting that they held luxury items available only to the richest of bears. The thought that some of those riches might have been used to buy his mother only increased Benjamin's determination to get them out of the trouble they were now in.

'We could climb on top of one of these crates,' he suggested. 'Maybe rats can't climb.'

'They *can*!' cried Mops at once, her voice rising in panic. 'Look!'

On top of the nearest crate, its little eyes gleaming, stood a fat, grey rat. Its nose was twitching as if it had just caught the scent of a tasty human. They watched, petrified, as it was joined by another – then another, crawling out from beneath the folds of a bale. Mops backed away across the puddled floor until she bumped into the crates on the other side of the hold-cargo.

'They're everywhere!' she screamed. On top of the crate she'd backed into were more pairs of pink gleaming eyes.

Benjamin tried to stay calm. 'I wonder how long this poison stuff they've put on us takes to work?' he said.

'Longer than it will take one of them to bite a lump

out of my arm!' Mops wailed. 'Think of something else! Something to get us out of here!'

'Mops, that could be it! How *do* they get things out of here?'

'The same way they dropped us down here, I suppose, by using ropes. Does it really matter?' Mops kicked out wildly at a bold rat that had crept close to her ankle. 'If we don't do something fast there'll be nothing left to pull up!'

Benjamin tugged at the length of rope leading out from his waist. It was loose at first, because he was pulling up the extra that was coiled up on the floor. But very quickly it tightened. He looked upwards – and saw why. After lowering them into the hold-cargo, the galley-bears must have left the ends of the rope outside and slammed the hatch shut down on them. He pointed this out to the increasingly panic-stricken Mops.

'So how's that going to help?' she screeched.

'It means we can climb up to the roof, Mops!' replied Benjamin. 'The rats won't be able to reach us there.'

'But they can jump, can't they!'

'Of course they can't! Come on!'

Feeding his rope through his hands until it was tight, Benjamin put one foot against the nearest crate and began to walk up it as though it were a wall. Reaching the top of the crate, he swung forward until his feet landed against the real wall of the hold-cargo. He carried on higher – and soon reached the roof. There he hung, his head close to the hatch, his feet braced against the very top of the wall. He was safe – for now.

'I can't do that!' wailed Mops.

She looked as though she meant it. Benjamin tried the only thing he could think of.

'Mops,' he said quietly, 'I can't quite tell from here. Are there three rats creeping up behind you or is it four?'

As he'd hoped, Mops didn't even look. With a squawk of terror she launched herself at the wall and began pedalling her legs as fast as she could while hanging on to her rope so tightly that her knuckes showed pure white. Moments later, Mops was dangling beside Benjamin.

'Well, sometimes I surprise even myself!' she chirped.

'Ssssshhh!' hissed Benjamin.

He'd heard the sound of a small drum. It had been rat-a-tatting steadily but, as Mops fell into a relieved silence, it quickly picked up speed to become a shrill drum-roll of fanfare. The moment it stopped they heard the unmistakeable voice of the galley-master bellow, 'Cheers-three for King Antonius and Queen Dearie! Hop-hop…'

A number of bears immediately responded with shouts of 'Ray-hoo!'

Two more hop-hops and ray-hoos followed. There then followed a variety of noises, ranging from paw-steps to gruff orders to chain-rattling. Exactly what had been happening up on the main deck Benjamin wasn't sure, but one thing seemed certain...

'That must have been King Antonius and Queen Dearie boarding the Galley-Royal,' he said to Mops.

'Then why don't we start screaming?' she said. 'Surely they'll haul us out if there's a chance we'll keep royalty awake!'

'I don't think so, Mops. They must have been expecting us to make a noise when they put us down here. Everybody must be used to ignoring the screams of trap-rats. Especially,' he added with a fearful glance down at the floor of the hold-cargo, 'as they probably don't scream for all that long.'

'Well, if it's no use screaming, think of something else!' cried Mops in frustration. 'We can't dangle here all night!'

Benjamin knew she was right. His arms were already aching badly. To give them a rest he would soon have to let himself back down into the depths of the puddled floor of the hold-cargo. He shuddered at the thought. The floor below him was now swarming with furry, pink-eyed rats.

Then from above them came the galley-master's gruff voice once more. 'Majesties-their aboard-are! Out-break the comb-honey-ration!'

'What's going on?' asked Mops.

'I think they must get a special treat to celebrate the king and queen coming on board the Galley-Royal,' said

41

Benjamin. 'Comb-honey is a very big treat. My owner, Mrs Haggard, always said so whenever she bought some. "Deserve-me treat-big," she'd say.'

Benjamin's arms were now hurting a lot. From the strained look on Mops's face he could tell that hers were hurting too. There was no getting away from it: soon they were going to have to drop down to the rat-infested floor. Suddenly they heard a galley-bear shout, 'Comb-honey-tub empty-is, Galley-Master!'

'Then another-get from hold-cargo!' the galley-master roared back impatiently. 'But forget-you-not plug-ears, Briny. Trap-rats-those soon-will screaming-be!'

'Aye-two, sir!' came the smart response, followed by rapidly fading paw-steps.

'Mops, did you hear that?' Benjamin said excitedly. 'Their tubs of comb-honey are down here. That galley-bear, Briny, must be on his way to get it.'

'Oh, wonderful!' wailed Mops. 'He's going to open this hatch, release these ropes, and send us plummeting to the floor to be eaten alive by that hoard of ravenous rats!'

Benjamin shook his head fiercely. 'No, he's not, Mops!' he said. 'That bear's paw-steps sounded as if they were moving *away* from us – which means there must be another way in to this place besides the hatch!'

And another way in meant another way *out*!

'Look around, Mops!' hissed Benjamin urgently. 'Can you see a tub with "comb-honey" written on it?'

In spite of her aching arms, Mops managed to get herself into a position with her feet almost on the ceiling and her head angled downwards. Then, trying to ignore the dozens of pairs of pink eyes which seemed to be peering straight up at her, she studied the bales and cases and tubs below.

'No,' she said as she read the paw-scratched markings on each, 'no, no, no, no, no, no...yes! See, that small round one beneath us? It was right under my nose all the time!'

'Perfect!' cried Benjamin. 'Now we've just got to hang on a bit longer, Mops – and not make any noise!'

'But won't that galley-bear expect us to be screaming?' objected Mops.

'Yes – so if we're quiet it'll confuse him. And a confused galley-bear is just what we want.'

So, hard as it was with their arms aching like mad, they made not a sound as a growing thump-thump of paw-steps was following by the clunk of a solid metal handle. A section of the far cargo-hold wall groaned open. In stepped a galley-bear, waggling the lantern in his paw to ward off any rats that might think of scurrying towards him. None did. At the sound of his arrival they'd all – as rats do – scurried back to their various hidey-holes to see whether the new arrival held out the prospect of danger...or dinner.

In the dim light Benjamin and Mops recognised the galley-bear as Briny, the one who'd coated them with the sticky rat-poison. He'd taken the galley-master's advice. Poking out from his ears were a couple of pine cones, perfectly shaped to block out the sounds of screaming trap-rats. Into the hold-cargo he padded, frowning as he looked this way and that as if he was (not surprisingly) expecting to see at least a few poisoned rats, not to mention some rather gruesome evidence of sap-chewing.

'Rat-traps?' Briny called softly, 'eaten-you ready-all?'

Like all bears who talked to saps, he wasn't expecting a sensible answer. But saps often did respond to the sound of a bear's voice, so the complete absence of any pitiful moans or wails of anguish – even after he'd unplugged his ears – came as a surprise.

Looking as confused as Benjamin had hoped, Briny was still looking around – everywhere but up towards the hatch – as he shuffled across the hold-cargo floor towards the comb-honey tub immediately beneath the dangling Mops.

'Now!' cried Benjamin.

As Briny bent towards the tub, Mops let go of her rope. Down she sailed, to land solidly on the galley-bear's furry head. Briny toppled forward with a groan, his confused brain wondering what kind of huge rat had just fallen on him. Dazed, he struggled back onto all paws – only to have the far-heavier Benjamin land on him.

Briny collapsed with a moan. Quickly, Benjamin

44

grabbed the galley-bear's lantern. Mops untied the rope around his waist. Benjamin untied the rope around hers. Finally, with the groaning Briny already beginning to stir, the two friends raced across to the hold-cargo door...and out.

THE ROOT-RUM BARREL

What they had to do now was to go up, up to the main deck. *With luck*, Benjamin thought, *they would be able to race across to the ramp and be down it to the quayside before any bear could move to prevent them.*

They'd emerged from the hold-cargo into a dark and gloomy corridor. A short distance along it, though, moonlight was spilling in from the stairway that Briny must have used to come down from the main deck. That had to be the way! Benjamin and Mops scurried to the bottom step and began to climb. Up the first flight they went, to a square landing. Another flight of steps rose beside them. The main deck was almost certainly at the top of these. Benjamin led the way.

What stopped him (so sharply that Mops almost ran into him) was the voice of the galley-master, not far above their heads, roaring, 'Off-cast! Ahead speed-full!'

It was this second command that told Benjamin they were too late to reach the ramp leading down to the quay-side. For at once a heavy drum beat began to thump – and the Galley-Royal started to move.

'Back down!' hissed Benjamin. 'We'll have to find somewhere to hide!'

Quickly they scampered down to the landing, desperately hoping that they wouldn't meet Briny racing up. They didn't – but from the furious grunts and growls coming from the direction of the hold-cargo it was clear it wouldn't be long before the galley-bear would be out to raise the alarm.

'There you are!' said Mops, pointing.

Just off the landing was a large, comfortable-looking alcove with a heavy curtain drawn to one side.

'Are you sure?' whispered Benjamin.

'Well, we're hardly knee-deep in alternatives, are we?'

Benjamin couldn't argue with that. Diving in to the alcove, they heaved the curtain across. It wasn't a moment too soon. Almost at once they heard Briny the galley-bear puff past. Mops risked a peek round the curtain.

'He's got that comb-honey tub on his shoulder…' she whispered, 'and what looks like a *very* big bump on his head.'

'Maybe he won't say anything in case he gets into trouble,' said Benjamin hopefully. 'You know, for letting us escape.'

Mops wasn't so sure. 'If that galley-master was expecting us to make a lot of noise then he'll be expecting to *hear* a lot of noise. And when he doesn't, he'll get suspicious and send somebody to investigate… or come down and take a look for himself!'

'What's the matter?'

Mops had made her last suggestion with a shrill squeak of panic, at the same time pointing a quivering finger at some writing gouged into the wooden wall of the alcove.

'That says "Galley-Master!"' she gulped. 'This must be his galley-den!'

The alcove certainly looked as though it might belong to a bear of some importance. Soft straw lay thickly across the floor, with an extra huge pile in one corner making a comfortable bed. Above this bed a huge hook jutted out from a solid beam. The hook had nothing hanging from it and Benjamin wondered briefly what could possibly be heavy enough to need a hook that size to hold it. Then his eye was taken by something else – something which looked far more interesting.

Attached to the alcove wall was an important-looking picture. At least it looked important to Benjamin, but as he couldn't read he wasn't absolutely sure. Mops, hopping up and down in her impatience to be gone, confirmed that it was.

'They're called plan-grounds. They show where the main cart-ways and dens are. My owner used to look at a little one before she went somewhere she hadn't been before. But that's a big one. That's a plan-town.'

'A what?'

'A plan showing the whole of Lon-denium. Look, it's even got the Under-Town stops marked on it.'

Benjamin shuddered. His one trip on the Under-Town had led to their capture and imprisonment in the Howling-Tower and he didn't like to think about it. Besides, his interest was elsewhere. He pointed at a long, wiggly blue thing on the plan. 'Is that a cart-way? It's a long one.'

'You wouldn't get far if you tried to walk on it,' said Mops. 'No, that's the Winding-River.'

Tracing the line of the river she read out the various places that it passed. 'See, it goes under Bridge-Lon-denium, past the Caverns of Prattlement – whatever they are – and on and on until...' She stopped, her mouth open and her eyes agog.

'What is it? Where else does it go?'

Mops jabbed a finger down on top of a large, round blob. It was right beside the Winding-River, but a long way off, at a point where the blue line had become very much thinner.

'Bearkingdom-Palace,' breathed Mops. 'That's where.'

Benjamin's heart leapt. What Roger Broadback had told them had to be right! 'Then we *must* stay on this Galley-Royal, Mops. My mother, Alicia, could be there in the palace.'

'In that case,' said Mops, moving towards the curtain which separated the alcove from the corridor outside, 'the sooner we find a safe hiding place the better – because something tells me that the galley-master's den is not it!'

Reluctantly, Benjamin moved away from the plan-town. Just looking at the blob marked 'Bearkingdom-Palace' made his mother feel closer somehow.

'Aha!' exclaimed Mops.

At the side of the alcove was a big, uncovered barrel, positioned so that it couldn't be seen even when the curtain was open. Mops was peering inside.

'What are you doing?' hissed Benjamin. 'I thought we were going?'

'First things first,' said Mops. 'I simply must wash off this revoltingly sticky poison-rat,' she said. 'I *dread* to think what it's doing to my skin. Leave it on much longer and I fully expect to come out in one gigantic rash. I'm not looking like a human raspberry if I can help it...' She beamed as she dipped a hand deep into the barrel and it came out dripping, '...and this seems to be the solution!'

'You can't wash in that – whatever it is,' hissed Benjamin.

'Root-rum, if my nose doesn't deceive me,' said Mops. 'That galley-master obviously follows the principle of treating his galley-bears with comb-honey and himself with root-rum.' She giggled. 'Just as well, I suppose. Comb-honey would have been perfectly *useless* for washing in!'

And with that, Mops plunged both her arms deep

into the barrel and swished them vigorously. Benjamin, seeing the sense in removing the poison-rat from their bodies, did the same. Both shook their arms, then finished drying them on the straw beneath their feet. Getting their legs into the barrel was a bigger problem.

'How about sitting on the edge and dangling them in?' suggested Mops.

And so it was that were both perched in that very position, swishing their sticky legs clean in the barrel of root-rum, when they heard a heavy clanking of keys approaching outside and the unmistakeable voice of the galley-master asking, 'Care-you-for a tot-little of root-rum, Chancellor Bruno?'

THE STARING MAN

Luckily, the barrel had only been about two-thirds full. This meant that, when they heard the galley-master coming, Benjamin and Mops could slide quickly off the rim of the barrel and down into the root-rum without the dark, strong-smelling liquid rising above their heads and drowning them. There wasn't much room to spare, though. The level of the powerful drink was up to their chests. They heard the curtain being swished back and two heavy sets of paw-steps rumble nearer.

'One-small me-for,' they heard Chancellor Bruno say.

'Keep-you-must head-clear, eh Chancellor?' chuckled the galley-master.

As they heard the voices, Benjamin and Mops sank down so that the dark liquid was well above their heads. Even so, had the galley-master looked into the barrel he couldn't have failed to see them. But he didn't. With a quick scooping motion, the bear dipped first one small drinking bowl, then a second, into the root-rum and out again. Moments later, Benjamin and Mops were rising silently back to the surface.

For a little while all they could hear was a gurgling in their ears. Then, slowly, low bear-voices became clear again.

'Happen-when?'

It was the galley-master, Benjamin was sure of that. It sounded as if he was whispering, though – a very difficult thing for any deep-voiced bear to do.

'Know-me-not.' Chancellor Bruno was trying to whisper too. 'When ready-all.'

'Need-me warning-some,' said the galley-master. The fat bunch of keys looped across his shoulder clanked as he moved. 'For fast away-gets need-me galley-saps-rested.'

'Will-you warning-get.'

'And King Antonius?'

Chancellor Bruno gave a throaty chuckle. 'Has clue-none!'

The galley-master chuckled too, then. 'Drink-me that-to!' They heard the sounds of slurping – then coughing. 'How-you-like the root-rum, Chancellor?'

Chancellor Bruno's voice seemed to have deepened further. 'Has-it...' he coughed, 'flavour-interesting...'

'More?'

'No-you-thank. Return-me-must to King Antonius... before decides-he more money-spends!'

Again the galley-master growl-chuckled nastily. 'Not-for longer-much. When King-you-become, money-spending decide-you-how!'

'Sssssshhh!' Chancellor Bruno sounded anxious.

'Nothing happen-can until reach-we Bearkingdom-Palace.'

'*If* reach-we Bearkingdom-Palace!' roared the galley-master suddenly. 'Galley-float-this is moving-hardly!'

Benjamin and Mops heard sounds of irritated movement, of drinking bowls being tossed aside and of heavy paws loping across the straw-covered floor. Then of claws, scratching on the bare wood of the corridor outside, growing softer as the two bears went their different ways. Where Chancellor Bruno went, they received no clue. Not so the galley-master. From a distance they heard him roar, 'Briny! Ordered-me speed-full, not paddle-slow! At speed-this not there-we-be till moon-next! Whip-you galley-saps-those!'

Benjamin slid back the lid of the barrel. He and Mops clambered out. They squeezed out their clothes, covering up the damp patches they made on the floor with dry straw from other parts of the galley-master's den. This took longer than expected because, for some reason, they both had difficulty in standing up straight.

When Benjamin tried to say, 'Do you think the poison-rat we washed into the root-rum will make the galley-master feel ill?' it took him two or three or sometimes four goes to get each word out right.

'I ho dope so,' said Mops with a silly snigger. 'I mean I do hope so.' She was swaying from side to side, a big smile on her face.

Both he and Mops had been careful not to swallow

any of the root-rum, but it had been impossible to avoid breathing in the powerful fumes in the barrel. Benjamin was feeling really light-headed – and it looked as if the same applied to Mops, only more so.

'We're off in a galley to Bearkingdom-Palace!' she trilled.

Benjamin hushed her loudly. 'Mops, be quiet!'

'Oh, phooey!' she snorted. 'Who's going to hear little me having a little sing when there's all that drumming going on?'

The thump-thump of the drum-beats had grown far louder. Faster, too. The thump-splash thump-splash sounds had also grown quicker, as if they were trying to keep in time with the drum. Whatever the galley-master had made Briny do, the Galley-Royal had definitely picked up speed.

The movement gave Mops even more trouble in standing. She slithered down to the floor, her back against the alcove wall, looking up at Benjamin with glassy eyes.

'Well, it looks like you've wish your got Jenmabin – I mean, Benmajin,' Mops slurred. 'Didn't you hear what the goggly-mister and Chunky Browno said?' She began singing again. 'We're off in a galley to Bearkingdom-Paaaalaaaace…'

Benjamin peered anxiously round the curtain, terrified that Mops's noise would bring a bear running to investigate. That thought alone was enough to make his head clear rapidly. He tried to get Mops to think serious thoughts to calm her down.

'Did you hear what they said about Chancellor Bruno becoming king?' he asked. 'How could that be?'

Mops shrugged. 'Who cares? Maybe they're going to have a contest. A singing contest!' She began trilling again. 'Old King Bruno played a merry old tunio – but Old King Antonius did nothing but groan-ius ...'

The racket forced Benjamin to take drastic action. Hauling Mops to her feet, he clamped one hand over her mouth and pushed her out of the galley-master's den with the other. They were immediately hit by a sudden blast of fresh air coming from the stairway they'd begun climbing – that is, until the sound of the galley-master's orders made them turn back.

Fresh air could be just what Mops needed. With luck it would not only help clear her mind but also help blow away the strong smell of root-rum wafting from them both. What's more, with the galley-float now on the move and the crew of galley-bears busy with whatever jobs they did, there would hopefully be less chance of them being spotted.

Still keeping his hand fixed over Mops's mouth, Benjamin guided her forward to the foot of the stairway. Side by side, they climbed one step...then another...until finally their heads rose above the level of the wide opening at the top...

'Oh, Mops,' gasped Benjamin in horror, 'this must be the galley-sap deck.'

Ahead, beside and behind them, were humans. They were seated in pairs on hard benches on either side of the aisle into which the stairway emerged. Gripped in their hands were long, heavy rowing-poles which stuck out through holes in the Galley-Royal's side. The wretched humans were heaving on these rowing-poles in time with the pounding drum.

Thump-splash-heave…Thump-splash-heave…Thump-splash-heave.

And with every heave the galley-saps were already groaning with effort – for the drum beats were growing faster. At the head of the aisle (and thankfully not looking their way) the galley-master had taken over the drumming from Briny. He was showing the bump-headed galley-bear the speed he wanted, shouting as he drummed,

'This-like! This-like!'

Benjamin had once seen a team of humans pulling an under-town slither-train and thought that was bad. This was far worse. The galley-saps were chained, both to their partner *and* to the benches they were sitting on. As for the deck on which they were imprisoned, this was almost completely enclosed. It had just one opening to let in fresh air. This was at the far end, where the galley-master was pounding on his drum. Every time the Galley-Royal surged forward, it brought a welcome gust of cooling air to the sweating, gasping galley-saps (which cleverly encouraged them not to slow down, of course, for then the fresh air died away).

Whether due to this small amount of fresh air, or to the horror of the sight before them, Mops began to recover from the effects of the root-rum fumes. At least she stopped wriggling and trying to prise Benjamin's hand from her mouth. Now she was wide-eyed – and pointing frantically.

Benjamin immediately realised why. Up ahead, having made it clear how fast he wanted the galley-saps to row, the galley-master was preparing to hand the drumming job back to Briny. Any moment now he'd be turning…leaving his place…and heading their way as he padded back to his den!

'Benjamin! Mops!' gasped a voice.

It came from close by, from the nearest of the two humans chained to a bench on their right.

'Roger Broadback!' hissed Mops (Benjamin having released his hand from over her mouth).

Even as he was heaving on the rowing-pole in front of him, the gangly young man was lifting his feet to reveal an inviting gap beneath his bench. Benjamin didn't hesitate. To go back the way they'd come was too dangerous. If the galley-master didn't stumble across them then somebody like Chancellor Bruno or Briny would. Besides, where they were now was closer to the top deck of the Galley-Royal. If and when it finally stopped they'd have less far to go in order to make their escape. And so, in one quick squirming movement, Benjamin dived up from the stairway and under Roger Broadback's bench.

Neither did he stop there. He wriggled on, so that Mops would have room to follow him in, until he was lying under the section of the bench occupied by Roger Broadback's rowing-partner.

'Thanks, Roger!' whispered Mops, the moment she was settled.

'Save it for later!' panted Roger Broadback as he rowed. 'Stay still and keep quiet!'

Mops curled herself into a ball. 'I wish that drummer would keep quiet,' she murmured. 'That thumping is going right through my head!' And with that, she jammed her fingers in her ears and was soon asleep.

Just as well, thought Benjamin. *It would give the effect of the root-rum time to wear off completely.* Until that happened there was always a chance that an irritated Mops might jump out and yell at Briny to keep the noise down. If they could only stay hidden where they were until the Galley-Royal reached Bearkingdom-Palace, then they'd have a chance of getting away.

If…

As time went on Benjamin began to feel increasingly uncertain about just how safe they were. It was the galley-sap beside Roger Broadback who worried him the most. As he'd dived beneath the bench,

Benjamin just had time to notice that Roger Broadback's rowing- partner was a grown man. As these two gasping galley-saps rowed, Benjamin had been able to see little more than the man's tough, wiry legs, stained with grime and sweat – the legs, something told him, of a man who'd been a galley-sap for a long while.

Now and again, whenever he had a spare breath, Roger Broadback had managed to gasp out a few words of encouragement. He'd told them to stay out of sight, keep well down, be alert. But – and this was the worrying thing – the man beside him hadn't uttered a single word. All he'd done, more and more often, was to lean forward and snatch the odd look at them. No, not at them – at *him*.

What was the man so interested in? Did he think that Roger Broadback's offer of shelter was going to get him into trouble? Benjamin didn't like to think what the punishment might be for a galley-sap caught doing something wrong. *Was the man just waiting for the right moment to raise the alarm and bring the galley-master running?*

A sudden growl from the front swept this worry aside for a moment. It came from the galley-master, returning to take charge.

'Down-slow!'

Briny's thumping drum-beat eased in response. As it slowed, so too did the heaving and gasping of the galley-saps.

'Thank goodness,' they heard the exhausted Roger Broadback breathe from above them, 'we must be nearly there.'

The drum-beat had slowed further. Now, to a roar from the galley-master of 'Stop-full!' the drumming ceased altogether.

'At last!' murmured Mops, unplugging her fingers from her ears and opening her eyes.

Finally released from their exertions, all the galley-saps slumped forward onto their rowing-poles. Cries of pain and weariness filled the air. Above Benjamin and Mops could hear Roger Broadback gasping. He showed no sign of looking beneath the bench to see how they were. The same went for the worrying man beside Roger — or so Benjamin thought, until he suddenly bent low in his seat to study Benjamin once more.

This time it was with a long, lingering look. With every moment that passed, Benjamin's stomach felt like it was being wound into knots. The man's mouth was opening. Was he going to shout out and reveal where they were hidden? The man was gasping with pain, trying to find the breath to speak — or shout...

'Benjamin.'

The man hadn't shouted. He'd spoken softly. Spoken *his* name. Confused, Benjamin looked into the man's eyes.

And he saw that those eyes weren't glowing with

suspicion – but love. Then memories came crowding back, of blissful evenings when he'd listened to wonderful stories of magical places like Hide-Park and huddled closer to the storyteller and looked into the same loving eyes he was looking into at that very moment.

'Father?' said Benjamin Wildfire, his heart bursting with joy. 'Oh, Father! Is it really you?'

AN IDEA-SPLENDID

For some moments, both Benjamin and his father, Duncan, were lost for words. After Benjamin had scrambled out from his hiding place beneath the bench, all they could do was remain locked in each other's embrace. Then the sounds of bustling and growl-shouting from the upper deck reminded them of where they were, and of the danger all around. Benjamin quickly crouched down out of sight.

'I didn't dare believe it was you,' whispered his father. 'But the more I looked, the more certain I was.' He smiled broadly. 'There can't be many boys with flaming red hair.'

Benjamin's hand flew to his head. Then the powerful smell of root-rum on his arms told him what must have happened – that the mud caking his red hair had been washed away along with the sticky poison-rat stuff. He gave his father another heartfelt hug. The touch of the cold, hard chains around Duncan Wildfire's waist brought tears to Benjamin's eyes.

'How did you get to be here?' he sobbed.

'After your mother and I came looking for you,' said Duncan Wildfire, 'we were caught and shut up in an evil place called the Howling-Tower. It was awful.'

'*Awful*?' said Mops, poking her head out from beneath the bench. 'That is an understatement! It was *terrible*! And that was just the food!'

'You were both in there too?' said a shocked Duncan Wildfire after Benjamin had quickly introduced Mops.

Benjamin nodded. 'We escaped, just like you. A trusty-sap named Twelve helped us.'

'And,' said Mops, 'he told us that your wife had been sold to a bear who could afford any price.'

'We guessed that could be King Antonius,' said Benjamin.

'Exactly what I thought,' said Duncan Wildfire. 'So I sneaked aboard this Galley-Royal, to try to reach Bearkingdom-Palace. But I got caught. And I've been chained here as a galley-sap ever since.'

Benjamin blinked back more tears. His father seemed so much older than he remembered him. His body looked thin and tired, and his red hair had grown so dull.

'Couldn't you have escaped?' he said. 'There must have been chances.'

Duncan Wildfire shook his head. He lifted his chain so that Benjamin could see the huge iron padlock attached to it.

'While the Galley-Royal's on the move, every one of us is chained down. Only when it stops do they let us up to do things like scrubbing the floors. But even then we're chained to the person next to us.'

Beside him, a glum Roger Broadback silently lifted his own padlocked chain for them to see.

'Couldn't you find a way of breaking it?' asked Mops. 'Benjamin once cleverly managed to escape from a chain by rubbing it with a sharp stone.'

Duncan Wildfire smiled on hearing this, but then shook his head. 'These chains are unbreakable, Mops. King Antonius can afford the best, remember. No, the only way of undoing them is by using a key...'

'The keys on the galley-master's shoulder-chain!' said Benjamin at once.

'Yes,' nodded Duncan Wildfire. 'And that's why it's been impossible to escape. Those keys and the galley-master are never apart.'

'Never?' frowned Mops. 'I find that very difficult to believe.'

Benjamin hissed like a snake. 'If my father says they're always with the galley-master then they *are*!'

As exhausted as he was, Duncan Wildfire found the strength to laugh. 'I see you haven't lost your spirit, Benjamin!'

'He seems to lose his powers of reason now and again, though,' snorted Mops. 'A family characteristic by the look of it.'

'I think you'd better explain yourself Mops,' said Roger Broadback.

'Certainly,' said Mops. 'I find it very difficult to believe that the galley-master and his keys are never apart for the simple reason that if they were always looped over his shoulder he'd never get a wink of sleep because they'd be digging into his ribs all night. In other words, I'd be very surprised if he didn't take them off at bedtime.'

'Mops – I'm sorry,' said Benjamin, his face turning almost as red as his hair. 'You're right, you must be.' Mops's reasoning had just given him the answer to a puzzle from earlier. 'That huge hook in the galley-master's alcove…'

'Just the right size for a gigantic bunch of keys,' nodded Mops.

Duncan Wildfire's eyes lit up. 'You've both been in there? You know the way?'

But before Benjamin or Mops could answer, a sudden noise from the far end of the galley-saps' deck sent them both scrambling frantically back beneath the bench and out of sight.

The noise – rather a rude and windy noise, if truth be told – had been made by the galley-master. He had reappeared, with Briny in tow. The smart grey bear was looking unwell. As he stalked down the aisle, he painfully clutched his middle.

'Got-me a guts-grumble,' they heard him growl to Briny. 'Going-me for a down-lie. Me-call when majesties-their are leave-ready.'

The root-rum, realised Benjamin. The poison-rat (not to mention the hair-mud) they'd swished into it might not have been powerful enough to do the galley-master any serious damage but it seemed to have been enough to badly upset his stomach.

Benjamin and Mops crept out warily from beneath the bench to see that Duncan Wildfire's eyes were more aglow than ever.

'Did you hear that?' said Benjamin's father. 'He's going for a lie-down. If Mops is right then he'll be taking off that bunch of keys and hanging them on that hook.' Desperately, he clutched at Benjamin's arm. 'My son, do you think you could try and get them?'

'Now?' frowned Roger Broadback. 'Won't there be galley-bears everywhere?'

Duncan Wildfire shook his head urgently. 'Not with King Antonius and Queen Dearie getting ready to leave. They'll all be up on deck to salute them, I'm sure. There'll never be a better time!'

It looked as if Benjamin's father was right. The rows of wheezing and exhausted galley-saps had been left completely alone. Not a single galley-bear was on guard. With the galley-saps all chained and shackled, they clearly thought that all was safe. So if he could get hold of those keys...and unlock every single padlock...

Benjamin leapt to his feet. 'I'm going to try, Father!' he said.

Mops was beside him in an instant. 'Excuse me. *We* are going to try.'

'No, Mops. It's best if I go alone.'

Mops sighed. 'I assume you saw the size of those keys? Drop one on your foot and you'll never walk again. It will take the two of us to carry them.'

And so, moments later, Benjamin crept down the stairway with Mops right behind him. Reaching the dark and gloomy corridor they paused. An encouraging sound had just come from the direction of the galley-master's alcove: the sound of metal keys clunking solidly against a wooden wall.

'Bet you he's just put them on the hook,' whispered Mops.

They waited, listening intently. Other sounds came their way now – disgusting, squelchy sounds – as the galley-master's stomach continued its tricks. Then deeper sounds, of heavy breathing. Finally, came the low rumbling noise of a snore.

Quickly they crept forward. The curtain had only been partly pulled across the galley-master's alcove. Benjamin and Mops peered through together. The miserable bear was sprawled out on his straw, his upset stomach cradled in his large paws. And looped over his shoulder and across his bulging middle was – nothing. Mops had been right. The galley-master *had* removed the huge bunch of keys. There they were, dangling from the hook directly above him. All they had to do was creep in and...

'Hoy!'

The angry roar stopped Benjamin and Mops dead. Swinging round, they saw Briny the galley-bear loping towards them. Having been told that King Antonius and Queen Dearie would be ready to leave quite soon, he'd followed his orders and gone to waken the galley-master.

'Run!' screeched Mops.

'Back-come, trap-rats!' roared Briny − who, though not the quickest thinker, had still managed to work out that if the two saps he could see in front of him were no longer in the hold-cargo then they might well be responsible for the painful lump on his head.

Unable to go back the way they'd come, Benjamin and Mops raced off in the only direction possible: down a further wooden stairway into the very depths of the Galley-Royal. Leaping from the bottom step, they skidded round a corner and found themselves in a damp and gloomy corridor, full of smaller alcoves (where the galley-bears lounged around when they weren't on duty, in case you were wondering).

They raced on, towards another stairway. This one led upwards. As they reached it, Benjamin risked a look back. Briny was still lumbering noisily after them. Much as it hurt to think that they were running further away from where he'd left his father, Benjamin knew they simply had to keep going.

Or had they? They'd gone *down* to the Galley-Master's

alcove, then *down* again to the dark corridor, then along, and now they were going up again. If they could keep going up, surely they'd reach the level of the galley-sap deck? ~~Yes – they'd come out at the other end, near the~~ opening! If they could get there well ahead of Briny they might just have time to race down the aisle and dive back beneath his father's and Roger Broadback's bench!

Benjamin flew up the stairs two at at time. He reached a landing, spun round a corner, then raced up more stairs towards an opening at the top. That *had* to be it!

'This way, Mops!' yelled Benjamin as he reached the opening and dived through.

'No!' screeched Mops.

She was too late. They had reached the other end of the galley-sap's deck. But what Benjamin hadn't suspected was that the galley-master, awakened by Briny's roaring, would have already come pounding up from his alcove.

'You-got!' snarled the galley-master as Benjamin ran straight into his sharp-clawed clutches.

'And you-got!' roared Briny, arriving in time to grab Mops.

Benjamin struggled and kicked. Mops screeched 'Let me go!' But there was no escape. With Duncan Wildfire and Roger Broadback watching helplessly from their chained-up places, Benjamin and Mops were hauled up to the main deck and across to the very side of the Galley-Royal.

'Them-drop river-in,' ordered the galley-master.

'Aye-two, Galley-Master!' replied Briny. 'With pleasure-much!'

The galley-master reared up on his hind legs. He growl-chuckled. There was nothing quite like throwing a sap into the river for making a bear with a sore head feel brighter. Powerless, Benjamin was lifted high into the air, as if the galley-master was going to try and throw him as far as he could. Far below, he could see the dark and filthy waters of the Winding-River swirling menacingly…

'What-here is on-going?' Benjamin heard a sharp bear's voice snap.

And then the most amazing thing happened. Instead of being hurled, Benjamin was lowered – not simply from above the galley-master's head, but right down onto the wooden planks of the Galley-Royal's deck. What was more, the galley-master then lowered himself as well, to kneel humbly beside him.

'Sap-drowning, Majesty-your,' he heard the grey bear mumble.

For a moment, Benjamin couldn't work out what was going on. Then what the galley-master had said sank in. *Majesty-your*?

He looked up. In front of the grovelling galley-master stood a she-bear with elegantly coiffured black fur. Not a strand was out of place. From both her wrists dangled glittering bracelets. Round her neck hung a chain of gold. And on her face was a look which showed that Queen Dearie was not amused. For that, Benjamin assumed correctly, was who had just spoken.

'Sap-drowning?' the queen now said, her voice rising. 'Ever-what for?'

'Faulty trap-rats, Ma'am,' said the Galley-Master.

'There-are-you, dear-my,' said another voice. 'Explained-all. Now along-come. Carriage-our awaits.'

The speaker stood a couple of paces behind Queen Dearie. King Antonius – for it was he – was tall and thin. He was immaculately groomed too, though it couldn't disguise the fact that he had far less fur on the top of his head than Queen Dearie. He made up for that by wearing a far heavier chain of gold round his neck.

'Then carriage-our wait-can!' snapped Queen Dearie. 'Ready-me-not.'

King Antonius turned to Chancellor Bruno who was standing by his side. 'She-bears!' he murmured (but not so loud that his wife could hear).

Queen Dearie may not have heard anyway. She had turned her attention back to the galley-master – though, as she spoke, she was looking intently at Benjamin Wildfire.

'River-throw a sap-handsome him-like? With valuable hair-red? Are mad-you?'

The galley-master's eyes flashed with anger, but he knew better than to answer back. He remained silent on his knees. Beside him, Briny had sunk so low before the

72

queen that his black snout was touching the deck. Seizing the opportunity, Mops wrenched herself free from him and ran straight into Queen Dearie's paws.

'How about me, then?' she trilled. 'I'm better than handsome! You should see me in purest pink!'

The queen may not have understand a word of Mops's squeaking but she obviously found it appealing. 'And one-this is sap-*gorgeous*!' she cooed.

'Heart-sweet,' said King Antonius patiently, 'Have-me meeting-important. Can go-we?'

The king was smiling. But then, Benjamin had noticed, he'd not stopped smiling at all, as if his smile was painted on his face. It didn't even fade when Queen Dearie cried, 'Have-me idea-splendid! Take-me saps-these to palace-our!'

'For use-what?'

'Show-saps!' said Queen Dearie. 'Train-me-them to prize-win!'

From behind the king, Chancellor Bruno gave a low growl of impatience. King Antonius shook his head.

'Idea-bad,' he said to the queen. 'They filthy-look… and body-stink!'

'Not-will-them after wash-good!' cried the queen. She gave the king a captivating smile. 'Oh, Tony-bear,' she cooed. 'Just me-for…'

Again King Antonius shook his head. 'No…' he began.

He got no further. Queen Dearie's dark eyes flashed.

Her tone changed to one that was needle sharp. 'Owe-you-me a hair-red!' she snapped.

This time King Antonius's smile *did* fade. For one brief moment it seemed to Benjamin as if a look of guilt crossed his face. Then it was gone and his smile had returned – but this time he was nodding.

'Well-very,' he sighed. 'Them-have if want-you.'

Queen Dearie gave a loud purr of delight. Folding Mops in her arms, she beckoned for the galley-master to release Benjamin. Then, handing them over to a couple of her helpers (known, they would discover later, as flunky-bears), the queen stalked regally off beside King Antonius towards the ramp leading down from the Galley-Royal.

'What do you think she meant by the king owing her a hair-red?' asked Benjamin as he and Mops were brought along behind.

Mops shrugged 'No idea.'

'Then how about her wanting to train us to be prize-winning show-saps?'

This time Mops did have an answer. 'Who cares? Being a show-sap has got to be better than being a drowned-sap!'

'That's true,' said Benjamin.

There was another advantage, too. They were going to face whatever lay ahead in Bearkingdom-Palace. And from what he'd just seen, it appeared that it was Queen Dearie who was the real ruler of Bear Kingdom. If she wanted something, it seemed that in the end King Antonius simply smiled and paid for it. Which meant that it might not have been him who'd bought his mother, Alicia, (if indeed that had ever happened) – but the queen.

Benjamin's mind was in a whirl. Against the pain he felt at leaving his father behind in chains was the hope in his heart that his mother could be there at Bearkingdom-Palace, waiting for him.

If he could find her... If somehow they could then get back to the Galley-Royal... If they could get hold of the galley-master's keys and set his father free...

It was with these thoughts racing around in his head that Benjamin found himself being led down the ramp towards a cart of glittering gold.

BEARKINGDOM-PALACE

Neither Benjamin nor Mops were to be given the chance to ride in this cart, however. Not even Queen Dearie would have wanted that until they'd been given a good clean up. The golden cart was for King Antonius and his wife alone. At its head, ready to begin pulling, were a team of cart-saps.

Mops looked at them with undisguised admiration. 'Well, if they're an example of how we're going to be looked after then I'll have no complaints!'

'We're trying to find my mother, Mops,' said Benjamin solemnly. 'Don't forget that.'

'Of course we are,' said Mops. 'But it won't do us any harm to be a little pampered while we're looking for her, will it?'

Benjamin couldn't argue with that. After the horrors of the Howling-Tower and the hold-cargo, the thought of being treated well was very appealing. And he had to admit that the cart-saps tethered at the front of the golden cart looked as if they'd been treated *very* well. They looked healthy and muscular, as if they had been given only the finest foods, and they were dressed splendidly, their uniforms of scarlet having not a patch or stain on them.

Beside the cart door stood a small bear with a ruffled collar in the same scarlet colour. This bear dutifully opened the door for the king and queen to clamber aboard. The royal couple took a few moments to get settled. Then, at a command from King Antonius, the cart moved off...to an eerie silence.

That was most unexpected. Benjamin had seen the crowds watching and waiting as he'd come down the ramp. He'd thought it strange that they weren't cheering but assumed the waiting bears – young and old – had simply been too full of wonder at seeing their king and queen. But for the watching bears not to make a sound even as the golden cart passed by...

'Shouldn't they be cheering?' he asked Mops after they'd been pushed up onto a second jet-black cart alongside a disgusted Chancellor Bruno.

'They *are* cheering,' said Mops. 'Listen.'

A low growl-cheer had begun to swell. Bear-spectators at the side of the paw-path had started waving. But most of them, it appeared, were waving not at the gold coach but at *theirs*.

'I think it must be me!' trilled Mops, waving back with small twiddly movements of her hand.

Benjamin quickly put her straight. 'It's not you at all. It's Chancellor Bruno they're waving at.'

That was certainly how it seemed. The chancellor was smiling and nodding – but not waving, as if that was only allowed for kings and queens. Benjamin suddenly realised why. It explained the strange conversation they'd overheard between Chancellor Bruno and the galley-master while they were hiding in the root-rum barrel.

'*When you king-become…*' the galley-master had said.

A plot was being hatched against King Antonius, it had to be. A plot that would mean Chancellor Bruno taking over as king. And from the reaction of the bears along the paw-path, having Chancellor Bruno become King Bruno would be highly popular. Until then, it seemed, the chancellor was being careful not to do anything to arouse King Antonius's suspicions – not even by waving back at those who were cheering him as he rode towards Bearkingdom-Palace.

A sudden sense of doom struck Benjamin as he remembered how Chancellor Bruno had answered the galley-master: '*Ssssshhh! Can nothing-happen until reach-we Bearkingdom-Palace.*'

What were they planning? What would happen to the king – and to Queen Dearie, for that matter? Most importantly, would it affect his own plans to try and find his mother?

Benjamin didn't get a chance to think further about these questions. For at that moment Mops hissed excitedly in his ear. 'We're here!'

'Already?' replied Benjamin. 'We've hardly moved!'

The tied-up Galley-Royal was still clearly visible back the way they'd come. Was it any wonder that King Antonius was unpopular if he threw away money by being carried even the shortest distances?

Benjamin looked out. The cart was passing through a gateway set in the middle of a long row of gold-tipped iron railings. Smart bear-guards snapped to attention as they went by. On they went, sweeping across a courtyard before stopping at the entrance to what Benjamin could only imagine was the largest and grandest den that any bear had ever lived in.

From the outside, Bearkingdom-Palace looked huge. But as Benjamin and Mops stepped through its pillared entrance they realised that appearances could be deceptive. Inside, the palace looked even bigger. Corridors stretched away in all directions. Gouged in gold on every wall were portraits of bear kings and queens reaching back as far as the earliest moons of Bear Kingdom. Gold flame-torches hung from every ceiling. And, sinking softly beneath their feet as they walked, rare ferns and flower petals carpeted every single patch of floor.

'This lot must have cost a fortune!' whispered Mops.

Benjamin could only nod. He'd been told that his mother, Alicia, had been bought by a bear who could pay any price – and you couldn't get a bear who fitted the bill more exactly than one who could afford to decorate his palace from top to bottom like this. Benjamin's heart pounded as they passed door after door, wondering each time: could she be behind this one...or this one...

Chancellor Bruno padded swiftly along the corridor to a splendid acorn-wood door with a huge crown claw-carved on its front. As King Antonius approached, Chancellor Bruno bowed deeply before swinging the door open to allow the king through. Benjamin just had time to see that a group of four large and serious-looking bears were already there waiting for him. This, he assumed, was the important meeting the king had referred to on the Galley-Royal, when he'd been asking Queen Dearie to hurry. The bears in the chamber did indeed look important. Each had a splendid chain around his neck. But that was as much as Benjamin saw. The moment King Antonius swept past, Chancellor Bruno followed him into the chamber and the door was swung firmly shut.

Benjamin and Mops now found themselves following Queen Dearie around corners and through corridors and up stairways until, finally, they were brought to a halt outside a pair of arched openings.

'Up-them-clean!' barked the queen, then swept off grandly.

Benjamin and Mops were now separated, each being led through a different archway by a different flunky-bear. They found themselves in the biggest, grandest sloshing-chambers that either of them had ever seen.

In Benjamin's case that wouldn't have been difficult. The only sloshing-chamber he'd known was the cramped alcove in which his previous owner, Mrs Haggard, had soaked herself in a sloshing-pool once a day and sluiced him down once a moon. But whereas her sloshing-pool amounted to no more than a scraped-out hole in the ground, this chamber had a massive, bear-sized bowl sunk into its centre. Mrs Haggard had only sloshed him with ice-cold water, but the water in this pool was steaming gently and smelled of fresh pine cones and wild honeysuckle. Stripped of his clothes and pushed in, Benjamin felt as if he was in the centre of a fragrant pond.

Mops clearly felt the same way, too. From the neighbouring chamber Benjamin could hear her squeals of delight: 'Oh, what luxury! Oh, what bliss!'

Benjamin's flunky-bear dipped him and sloshed him and used her claws to scrape the layers of grime from his skin. This stung, but when it was all over Benjamin felt cleaner than he'd ever felt before. His red hair was then washed until it shone. Finally, he was lifted out of the bowl and dried with wads of the fluffiest moss. Squirts of an expensive, perfumed potion that old Mrs Haggard would have given her right paw to have afforded, topped things off.

Benjamin was now dressed. His filthy orange outfit

was taken away, the flunky-bear doing this with one paw as she held her snout with the other. In its place Benjamin received a sap-suit of the finest blue silk. Then his red hair was combed carefully. The flunky-bear did this with her claws, of course, carefully teasing out the knots and snags.

At the end of all this, Benjamin was guided back out into the corridor. He found Mops there waiting for him.

'Oh, look at you!' she cried. 'More important, look at me!'

Mops, too, had been washed and pampered. Her skin shone and her eyes glowed. She'd been given sap-clothes in her favourite pink colour.

'Very pretty, Mops,' smiled Benjamin.

'*Pretty*?' she squawked. 'Is that all you can say? How about glamorous? Or gorgeous? Dazzling, even? Or stunning or bewitching or sensational or eye-popping or—'

'Yes, yes!' interrupted Benjamin. 'All of them.'

'Well, excuse me if I say that you don't sound very convincing. Nor happy, for that matter. Here we are in heaven and look at your face. I haven't seen a face as gloomy as that since…well, since that misery Spike ran off.'

Their two flunky-bears had taken them by the wrist and were leading them along yet another winding corridor to some place deep inside Bearkingdom-Palace. Mops was right. Benjamin did feel miserable. The sheer size of the palace had been the cause.

'It could take ages to find my mother in this place,' he said.

Mops smiled. 'Don't worry, we'll find her. And look on the bright side – at least we'll be well looked after in the meantime!'

Benjamin tried to smile back, but failed. He had another worry, one that it seemed silly to mention.

'What are we going to have to do to earn all this?' he said.

'Does it matter?' cried Mops, showing that she thought the worry was just that – silly. 'Benjamin, we've been bathed. We've been dressed in all this finery. Who *cares* what we have to do!'

SAP-TRAINING

They weren't to find out what was wanted of them until over seven sun-comes later.

By then, Benjamin and Mops were becoming used to their new quarters. They were as different to the cell they'd shared in the Howling-Tower as could be. Instead of cold iron bars, the walls of this chamber were made out of fragrant pine wood. It wasn't cold and gloomy, but light and airy. And it certainly wasn't cramped. Although the chamber was occupied by at least a dozen other perfumed and pampered boys and girls, each of them had their own private section containing a fluffy, sweet-smelling bed.

All this might have been expected. One further difference had surprised Benjamin a lot, though: the quiet. In the Howling-Tower there had always been somebody crying with hunger or calling for help or encouraging a neighbour to keep going. Here, apart from a few nods and smiles and the occasional 'good sun-come', none of the other children seemed to want to talk much. But, strange as he found this, Benjamin didn't much mind. The last thing he wanted was for his intention to search for his mother, Alicia, to slip out.

As for Mops, she appeared not to mind the peace and quiet in the slightest. She'd dived straight into her bed and had hardly left it since.

'Mmm…' she purred, her eyes closed as she wriggled her toes deeper under the covers, 'this is the life for me!'

'You don't really mean that?' whispered Benjamin.

'Mean it?' echoed Mops. 'Of course I mean it! Well, what I mean is…no. Not really. Only until we find…'

'Ssssshhh!' hissed Benjamin, glancing around the chamber. But none of the others were listening. They were all too busy preening themselves. The flunky-bears were due.

These two bears – who they'd discovered were named Cringe and Simper – arrived just after every mealtime. They would choose one or two of the children there and take them away. These children would be returned before the next meal-time, when the pattern would be repeated. Benjamin and Mops had yet to be chosen.

Benjamin edged closer. 'I was thinking we could try looking round if we don't get chosen.'

Much as he'd been wanting to, Benjamin hadn't yet ventured out. Bearkingdom-Palace was so huge that he'd been afraid he and Mops would get hopelessly lost. Instead, he'd tried to draw a map in his head whenever the flunky-bears took them for their daily bathe and change of clothes. This had been quite possible, because they'd been taken to a different sloshing-chamber almost every time. Bearkingdom-Palace appeared to have dozens of them.

'Look around?' echoed Mops, quietly this time. 'Anywhere in particular? Somewhere…well, *food-related* would be a bonus.'

It had been a strange thing. With all the luxury around, Benjamin had been expecting lavish meals to be served up too. But no. The food-bowls they were served with at mealtimes were really rather small. The roots and berries they'd held had been beautifully fresh and tasty, no question about it, but every meal would end with them both hungry for more. They were about to discover why.

Cringe and Simper arrived, as usual, not long after. The moment they entered all the other boys and girls immediately sat up straight, their arms folded across their chests. One even had his folded arms up by his nose, so eager was he to attract the flunky-bears' attention. But they were all ignored. This time the two flunky-bears had come for Benjamin and Mops.

They were led, not along the winding corridors of Bearkingdom-Palace, but outside to the palace's massive rear garden. Benjamin's heart sang as he saw the swathes of grass and the towering trees. Maybe they were going to be allowed to run and climb!

Lolling in the shade of one of the trees was Queen Dearie. Behind her, one flunky-bear was waving a leafy branch to keep her cool. Another was dipping wild fruits into a dish of honey and dropping them into her opened mouth. A third flunky-bear was smoothing her outstretched claws with a golden file. But the moment the queen saw Benjamin and Mops all this ceased.

'Ooh, at-them-look!' cried the queen, scattering the servants with a wave of one paw. 'They *gorgeous*-are!'

In his silk sap-suit Benjamin didn't feel gorgeous, he felt stupid. Mops clearly felt differently. 'You are *so* right, your Majesty!' she trilled, 'Gorgeous is the word!'

Cringe and Simper smiled and bowed. Praise for the saps was praise for them. They prodded Benjamin and Mops closer to Queen Dearie.

'So – am-they clever-also wonders-me?' said the queen eagerly. 'Know-them commands-any? Shall-me out-find!'

She rolled her fat body into an upright position. Then, looking Mops straight in the eye, she commanded, 'Down-sit!'

'It will be a *pleasure*!' responded Mops and immediately squatted on the warm grass.

'Understands-she!' cried Queen Dearie, clapping her paws in delight. She thought for a moment. 'Another-me-try...legs-cross!'

'As good as done,' said Mops and, to the queen's great glee, crossed her legs elegantly.

'What are you doing?' hissed Benjamin.

'She thinks she's training me to obey her commands,' said Mops. 'Didn't your Mrs Haggard ever do any training on you?'

'No.'

'*That* I can believe,' sniffed Mops. 'Well, my owner did training with me. And if there's one thing I learned about training it's that if you do what you're asked then...aha! Here they come!'

While Mops had been captivating the queen, Cringe and Simper had padded across to a cool and shaded nook. Now they were heading back again, laden with trays of sweet-smelling food.

'What have they got?' asked Benjamin, although his nose was already telling him the answer.

'Treats,' replied Mops. '*That's* what I learned. Obey a command, get a treat!'

And, sure enough, the moment the trays arrived, Queen Dearie speared a juicy piece of fruit with a sharp claw and gave it to Mops.

'I bet you *that's* why we get small helpings,' slurped Mops. 'So that we're keener to earn treats.' She snatched at another that Queen Dearie was offering. 'And I am!'

The queen then turned to Benjamin. 'Am-you hair-bright,' she said, looking at him with narrowed eyes, 'but am-you brain-bright?' She jutted her black snout forward until it was almost touching Benjamin's nose. Then she said sharply, 'Down-sit!'

Benjamin remained standing.

'Down-sit!' repeated Queen Dearie.

Benjamin didn't move.

'Down-sit! Down-sit! Down-sit!' shouted the queen.

'What are you doing?' cried Mops. 'Just sit down like she says.'

'No!' snapped Benjamin. 'I'm not doing tricks just to keep her happy.'

'Don't be silly—'

'No!'

Queen Dearie, to whom all this talk was just unintelligible sap-squeaking, had been growing visibly angrier. Now she roared at Benjamin one more time, 'Down-sit!'

Yet again, Benjamin stubbornly refused to move. But this time he had no choice. At a signal from the queen, Cringe and Simper lifted Benjamin high into the air before thumping him down in a sitting position. Then, as Cringe held his mouth open, Simper stuffed a treat in.

'Sap-good,' growled Queen Dearie.

Benjamin tried to get up again, but Cringe was still holding him down. Queen Dearie barked out her next command, 'Legs-cross!'

Before he'd had a chance to disobey, Cringe took one leg and Simper the other. Digging their claws into the backs of his thighs they then changed places. As his legs were twisted into position, Benjamin cried out in pain.

'Sap-good,' growled Queen Dearie again, though it was clear from the scowl on her face that she didn't mean it. This time Benjamin didn't even get a treat.

'Oh, Benjamin,' pleaded Mops, 'just do what she says.'

'No!' shouted Benjamin angrily.

And so it went on. Mops would unfailingly obey every new command that the queen issued. 'Up-stand!' saw her leaping to her feet to pose gracefully, her head cocked prettily to one side. 'Flop-belly!' and Mops was rolling onto her front, this time to support her chin with cupped hands.

She even responded to 'Toe-tip!' by skipping in a circle on the tips of her toes with her legs straight and her arms delicately outstretched.

Benjamin stubbornly resisted every time. And, every time, Queen Dearie had Cringe and Simper force him to do what she wanted. By the end of the session he was blinking back tears of pain.

'Look at you,' said Mops when they were finally taken back to their luxurious quarters. 'Battered and bruised. And all because you're too proud to look silly.'

'Unlike some people,' muttered Benjamin.

'Unlike some *clever* people,' hissed Mops. 'And shall I tell you why? Because by doing what the queen wants, it will make her like me. If she likes me she'll want me to be with her more often. The more often I'm with her, the more I'll discover out about what goes on in Bearkingdom-Palace. And the more I find out about this place, the more chance I'll have of finding out what happened to your mother, Benjamin Wildfire!'

Benjamin flushed red with shame. 'Oh, Mops. I'm sorry. I thought you were just doing it for the treats.'

Mops shrugged. 'Well, I'm not saying they weren't a bonus – but that's all they were.'

'You're sure?'

'Absolutely. Definitely. No doubt about it.' She smiled to herself. 'I wonder what they'll have next time...'

She didn't have long to wait. Before the next middle-sun, Cringe and Simper took them out into the palace gardens again. This time Benjamin tried far harder. He sat down and stood up and crossed his legs whenever Queen Dearie commanded. He couldn't do it with the same cheerful enthusiasm as Mops – she obeyed every command with a smile and a squeal of pleasure – but at least he did them well enough to escape punishment.

Benjamin even found there was one command that he'd obey willingly. It was, 'Here-come!'

Whenever Queen Dearie used it, they were supposed to run straight to her side. This, Benjamin quickly realised, meant that they got the chance to wander around and explore. So long as he always ran back to Queen Dearie the moment she called then she was happy.

'And we get a treat into the bargain!' beamed Mops.

They began cautiously, wandering no further than the little shaded nook. Then, the moment they heard 'Here-come!' they ran back, with Benjamin trying to look as if he was enjoying himself. Gradually they wandered further and further...and made a curious discovery.

Dotted here and there around the huge garden were figures on little pedestals. Whenever they repeated the 'here-come' exercise, Benjamin headed for a different one. He saw that some of the figures were proud, upright bears. Some showed birds and other creatures. The curious discovery was that there were also a couple of particularly beautiful *human* figures.

'What are they?' Benjamin asked Mops.

'Never-moves,' answered Mops. 'They're made out of stone.'

'They don't look quite right,' said Benjamin, although he couldn't for the life of him think why.

'Perhaps because they don't move?' said Mops. 'And we do?'

Benjamin was pretty sure that wasn't it, but he didn't feel like arguing. Mops knew so much more than he did about so many things.

'Here-come!'

Queen Dearie's screech carried across the garden. Benjamin didn't hesitate. The thoughts he'd been having – about what the never-moves were actually *for* – were swept away as he turned and raced back, arriving a long way ahead of Mops as usual. The queen even ruffled his red hair as she growled plummily, 'Sap-good. Better-getting.'

Benjamin smiled to himself. One day she was going to think differently. One day she'd scream 'Here-come!' until her eyes popped out and he wouldn't come:

because that would be the day he found his mother.

She was here somewhere. He was certain of that. All he could hope was that Mops's plan to get closer to Queen Dearie would help them find out where...

THE CREATURE

Mops's plan was working. Partly.

She was becoming one of Queen Dearie's favourites, that much was certain. For the next few sun-comes, Cringe and Simper would regularly turn up and take Mops away on her own.

'I'm getting extra training!' Mops said breathlessly when she returned the first time.

Benjamin didn't ask what the training was. There was only one thing he wanted to know. 'Did you find out anything?'

'I found out where the queen's chambers are,' said Mops. 'Down and along and up and round a corner – or was it two corners? – oh, I'm hopeless at directions…'

'I mean, did you find out anything about my mother!'

Mops shook her head. 'No. Sorry.'

The time after, she reported on how the Bear Kingdom's finances worked. 'Apparently there are four important bears called bearons who look after the four quarters of Bear Kingdom. They must have been the bears we saw waiting for King Antonius the day we arrived. Anyway, they collect money from all the bears living in their quarter. It's called in-claw tax apparently. Anyway, it's Chancellor Bruno's job to collect all this money and give it to King Antonius.'

'Who then gives it to Queen Dearie, I suppose,' said Benjamin impatiently.

'Nowhere near enough, according to her. She spent most of my training session moaning about needing more keeping-palace money.'

'But did you find out anything about my mother?' Benjamin managed to ask at last.

Mops paused. 'No-o,' she said finally, 'nothing useful, I'm afraid.'

The next time was just the same. Mops began babbling before Benjamin could even ask about his mother. 'There's going to be a really big event soon!' she cried. 'A banquet! Anybear who's anybear will be invited...'

Benjamin lost patience with her. 'I don't care about any silly banquet! I don't care about how the Bear Kingdom works or what tricks you're being trained to do. Mops, all I care about is what's happened to my mother! That *is* why we're here, remember! Now have you heard *anything* about her?'

Mops lowered her eyes. She shook her head slowly. 'No. I – I haven't heard anything...' She glanced up at

Benjamin, then lowered her eyes again. '...anything that will help you find her. Sorry.'

Benjamin lay awake all night. He didn't doubt that Mops was doing her best, but he couldn't wait any longer. He was going to search for himself. He would do it the very next time Mops was taken for training without him.

He didn't have long to wait. Straight after their next sun-come mealtime, Cringe and Simper arrived to take Mops off to Queen Dearie. Moments later – with the other sap-pets all too busy combing their hair and looking at themselves in a glass-shiny to notice – Benjamin slid out into the corridor.

Not knowing where to begin looking in the enormous palace, he decided to put his trust in luck. He would turn right, then left, then right, then left and so on. At least that way he'd have no difficulty in remembering how to get back again.

As he crept his right-left way along the corridors, shrinking back into one of the many nooks and crannies whenever he heard a bear approaching, Benjamin thought hard. What sort of job might King Antonius have made his mother do? Nothing that needed strength, almost certainly. The bears seemed only to force ghastly tasks like being a cart-sap or a galley-sap onto strong humans like Roger Broadback and his poor father. And girls like Mops seemed to be used mostly as pet-saps.

But what about grown-up girls, like his mother, Alicia? Number Twelve, the trusty-sap in the Howling-Tower, had called her: *'The most beautiful woman I've ever seen'*. What might the bears use beautiful women for? Gentle jobs, perhaps, such as strewing the fragrant ferns and petals with which the palace corridors were always freshly-carpeted?

Still engrossed in his thoughts, Benjamin suddenly found that he'd right-lefted as far as a large, square space with passageways leading off in all directions. The space was brightly lit but, fortunately, deserted – apart, that is, from a never-move figure right in its centre. It was that of a woman, posed in Queen Dearie's favourite legs-cross position. Her body was stony grey, her hair a lustrous brown. Once again, just as when he'd seen the never-moves in the palace garden, Benjamin got the feeling that something about the figure wasn't quite right. But suddenly he wasn't thinking about never-moves at all. For he'd heard a piercing cry of pain coming from somewhere; somewhere *beneath* him!

He hurried past the never-move to the other side of the square space. Here a wide archway led through to a torch-lit passageway. Now the cry came again, louder, this time followed by a bear's angry roar. Benjamin scurried on, to find the passageway dividing into two. One part circled away to his right, the other to his left, before meeting again on the far side. But...on the far side of *what*? From where Benjamin was standing it looked like a brightly glowing hole!

Again the cry came, almost a shriek this time. It had come from deep in the hole. Sinking to his stomach, Benjamin slithered forward, ever closer, until finally he could peer over the edge…and down.

He was looking into a high-walled pit. The walls were lined with torches. At the bottom was a small circle of dusty ground. And there, grovelling in the dirt as it cried with pain, was a creature beyond his imagining. Its head was the head of a bear. The sharp claws jutting viciously out from the ends of its arms and legs were the sharp claws of a bear. But those arms, those legs, and the rest of the creature's body was unmistakeably that of a human.

The creature wasn't alone. A rugged bear with short-cropped fur was by its side, cuffing it and shouting angrily. Looking on bleakly from behind them both stood King Antonius.

At the king's command, the rugged bear dragged the creature to its feet. Then he began jabbing it with his claws and swaying away, almost as if he was trying to make the creature angry enough to chase after him. But all the creature did was slump to its knees before crawling across the floor to cower pathetically against the pit's sheer wall.

It was King Antonius who brought the awful scene to a merciful end. 'Enough!' he shouted at the rugged bear. 'Use-him-none! Drag-away and him-sell!'

As the poor creature was hauled out of the pit, King Antonius lashed out at the wall with his paw, leaving gouge marks in the clay.

'How-me another-find?' he roared furiously. '*Where*-me another-find?' Angrily he swung round, looking up as he did so towards the rim of the pit high above him. And he saw…nothing.

Stricken with terror at the scene he'd just witnessed, Benjamin had already turned and started to race back along the passageway. Bursting out into the square space he didn't look or care if there was any bear around. There was only one thought on his mind: to get away from this awful place as fast as he could. Through the archway he raced, only to find he couldn't remember whether his first turning should be to the right or the left. In the event he did neither. Instead, as he tried to slow down, he lost his balance and hurtled slap-bang into the never-move sitting crossed-legged on its pedestal.

And to his utter astonishment he heard it say irritably, 'Watch where you're going, young man.'

ROSETTA WILLOWTHIN

Stunned, Benjamin could only stop and stare. He'd run into the never-move woman with such force that he'd knocked her sideways. She was now arranging her limbs back into the cross-legged position in which he'd first seen her. Within moments she'd done it and was looking once again as if she was made of stone.

'You're...*r-real*?' stammered Benjamin.

The never-move didn't answer.

Benjamin glanced anxiously back towards the archway leading to the pit. The corridor beyond was still deserted. Heart pounding, Benjamin forced himself not to race on. Instead, he reached out a finger and pressed the never-move's arm. It was warm. And his finger sank into it slightly.

'You *are* real!' he said. 'You're not made of stone at all. You're made of skin and bone, just like me.'

'Ssssshhh!' hissed the never-move urgently. 'Do you want to get my pretty head cut off? Because that's what will happen if I'm seen talking to you!'

Breathlessly Benjamin checked along all the corridors

leading into the square area. 'No bear's coming,' he said. 'Please – tell me who you are. What are you doing here?'

'Go away!' muttered the never-move.

'No!' hissed Benjamin. 'Not until you answer me!'

The never-move sighed. Then, arranging her face into a fixed expression, she whispered through parted lips, 'My name is Rosetta Willowthin. I am a never-move. My job is to bring beauty to the palace. Every day my skin is painted to look like stone. I then climb up onto this pedestal...*and shouldn't move!*' she emphasised anxiously.

Benjamin was shocked. 'But that's an awful way to live.'

'No, it's not,' said Rosetta, 'it's a great honour. King Antonius only buys the most beautiful humans for never-moves.'

The most beautiful? Once again, the words of Twelve, the Howling-Tower trusty-sap, sizzled across Benjamin's mind: *Alicia Wildfire. The most beautiful woman I've ever seen.*

'Rosetta! Do you know a never-move named Alicia? Alicia Wildfire?'

'Yes, I do,' said Rosetta.

She'd said the words so simply, so quietly, that for a moment it didn't sink in. When it did, Benjamin could hardly contain himself.

'She's my mother!'

Rosetta permitted herself the merest nod of her head. 'Ah, yes. Red hair.'

Even as she said this, Benjamin was finally realising what it was about the never-moves that hadn't seemed quite right. He couldn't believe he hadn't noticed it before. Although their skins had been painted to look like stone, their hair had been left as it was. Rosetta Willowthin's deep brown curls were their rich, natural colour.

'Rosetta, is my mother somewhere in the palace? Can you tell me?'

This time, Rosetta's head gave the slightest of shakes. 'I can only tell you where she *was*,' she said. 'She was *here*. On this pedestal.'

'Here?' gasped Benjamin. Misty-eyed, he briefly ran his fingers over the rough stone. 'Then why isn't she here now?'

'I don't know!' exclaimed Rosetta, shaking her head in exasperation at this non-stop questioning. She immediately stiffened into her best never-move pose. Her lips hardly parted as she hissed, 'Now go away!'

Benjamin hurriedly checked all the passageways again. They were still alone. He then strode back to stand so solidly in front of Rosetta that he might have been mistaken for a never-move himself. 'I'm going nowhere,' he said, arms folded, 'until you tell me all you know.'

Rosetta's eyes flickered irritably. Then, realising that Benjamin meant what he said, she sighed and spoke again.

'It happened after the last Banquet-Royal,' she said

102

quickly. 'I was on my pedestal in the garden, a lovely one with lots of pretty yellow flowers painted on it. Out came King Antonius, Chancellor Bruno and all the bearons. The King looked furious. They stood and stared at me. Then one of the bearons – don't ask me which one, they all look the same to me – said, 'No. Want-me the hair-red.' That was it. Next sun-come I was brought in here. And that *is* my final word,' she snapped.

Benjamin looked at Rosetta. The never-move had stiffened her neck. Her lips were set in a firm line. She was gazing blankly into space. She meant it, knew Benjamin. He'd not persuade her to speak again.

But what did it all mean? The talk of bearons and the Banquet-Royal made him wish he'd listened to Mops more carefully when she'd been telling him what she'd found out. For now, though, he could only come up with one answer – that the bearon in question had been telling King Antonius that he wanted his mother Alicia to be swapped onto a pedestal outdoors. In the garden!

'Thank you, Rosetta!' he whispered. 'Thank you!'

Wildly, hardly able to breathe at the thought, Benjamin began racing left-right-left-right back the way he'd come.

Behind him, Rosetta Willowthin added one final movement to her final word. A single tear trickled down her cheek as she sighed from the bottom of her always-moving heart.

BENJAMIN'S REBELLION

Benjamin arrived back just in time. No sooner had he caught his breath than Simper and Cringe turned up to take him out into the garden. Mops was already there, curled up at Queen Dearie's feet. The queen was gabbling at her in an odd, coo-growling kind of voice.

'Pinkie-pops,' she said, patting Mops on the head. 'Am-you my pupil-star! Doing-you full-wonder with training-extra am-you!' She gave Benjamin a look of scorn as he was led into her presence. 'But sap-this needs-still work-more!'

'Pinkie-pops?' Benjamin couldn't resist echoing, with a snigger.

'It's her sap-pet name for me,' shrugged Mops. 'She likes me. She'll like you too, if you do what she asks.'

Benjamin hoped Mops was right – and she was. As he proceeded to obey the queen's every command flawlessly and with a forced smile her attitude did change. By the time Benjamin had sat down and stood up and crossed his legs and tip-toed every time he'd been asked, she was beaming with pleasure. Finally the moment arrived that all this good behaviour had been leading towards: the time when Queen Dearie allowed them to wander away on 'here-come!' practice. Benjamin had noticed she gave a longer wander to those who'd behaved the best – and a long wander was just what he wanted.

Benjamin had been intending to first tell Mops what he'd seen in the pit and heard from Rosetta Willowthin, but he was simply too agitated. Instead, now that the time had come, all he could do was cry excitedly, 'I think I know where my mother might be!' before hurrying off ahead.

What he was looking for was the pedestal Rosetta had described, with yellow flowers painted on it. In all their previous wanderings round the Palace garden – and they'd been to most of it – he'd never seen one like that. There was one place they hadn't been to before, though. Shielded by a claw-clipped hedge with an archway in the centre, it was like a garden within the garden. Until now, Benjamin had only looked through the archway from a distance and seen the ruler-straight paw-paths of coloured stones and the flower beds of different shapes. This time he intended to go inside.

'Benjamin! Wait!' cried Mops, still some way behind. 'Don't!'

Benjamin took no notice. He plunged through the archway. Stones scrunched beneath his feet as he hurried along the nearest paw-path. Desperately, he looked around. He could trees and shrubs, lolling corners and scratching-posts, but no pedestals! And then, suddenly, he saw it. At the very centre of a semi-circular grotto there stood a never-move's pedestal decorated with the loveliest painted yellow flowers, just as Rosetta Willowthin had described it.

It was empty.

'Oh, Benjamin—' said Mops, arriving at his shoulder.

Benjamin whirled round. Hot tears coursed down his face. 'Don't "Oh Benjamin" me!' he shouted. 'This is where she should have been!'

Then he told her the story of his meeting with Rosetta Willowthin, and what he'd learned about his mother and King Antonius and the unknown bearon who said that he wanted the hair-red never-move.

And at the end of it Mops said quietly, 'I know.'

'You know?' gasped Benjamin. 'How?'

'Well I didn't know *exactly*. But when Queen Dearie talked about the Banquet-Royal they're having soon she also mentioned a favourite hair-red never-move. She said she lost her at the last banquet because of the king.'

A memory shot into Benjamin's mind: of the queen snapping at the king when they were on the deck of the Galley-Royal, '*Owe-you-me a hair-red!*'

'Why didn't you tell me!'

Mops was looking embarrassed and hurt at the same time. 'Because I wasn't certain she was talking about your mother and if she was I didn't want to make you feel awful and…and…' Her voice had faded to a whisper.

'You knew if my mother wasn't here I'd want to run away again, didn't you?' he said sharply. 'And you don't want to leave.'

Mops snorted. 'Benjamin Wildfire, that is ridiculous. Of course I want to leave…but not until the time is right…'

'Here-come!'

Cutting through the air came the silly, high-pitched voice Queen Dearie used when calling them to her side.

'This *is* the right time!' shouted Benjamin angrily.

'No, it is not!' retorted Mops. 'Not until my extra training is finished.'

'Extra training. To do what, stand on your hands?'

'No, to *write*!'

As she said it, Mops raised her right index finger in the air for Benjamin to inspect. It was slightly blue-stained and its nail had been filed to a flattened point.

'You've seen the way the bears do it,' continued Mops, 'by dipping one sharp claw into a pot of ink-blue. Well, now I can do the same! I've already learned how to write my name!'

'Why?' snapped Benjamin. 'Can't you remember who you are any more?'

'That is *unfair*! I'm doing it for us! Learning how to

write could be really useful when we do run away from here.'

'Why?'

'Er…because…' stammered Mops, '…it just will be! And anyway, we can't go now. We haven't collected supplies or anything…'

'Are you sure that's the reason? It couldn't be because you're enjoying it here?'

'No! I mean, yes! Oh, you're confusing me!'

'Here come!' called Queen Dearie again, this time in an angry roar.

Mops said no more. She just turned and ran, her pink outfit rustling around her legs as she sped across the grass. Benjamin didn't follow. He wasn't going back. He was going to run, away from Bearkingdom-Palace, right now, at this very moment!

And do what? he then thought. Get back on board the Galley-Royal, attack the galley-master, grab his keys, outwit all the galley-bears and set his father free from his chains? All on his own? His heart sank. It couldn't be done, not on his own – and certainly not right now. Much as he didn't want to admit it, Mops had been right: now wasn't the time.

'Here-come!!' bellowed Queen Dearie once more.

So Benjamin went. Slowly, dragging his feet, and with a burning anger in his heart – but he went.

'Sap-good,' sniffed the queen as he arrived, and tossed him the tiniest treat she could find.

She then turned her attention back to Mops. She was sitting on the ground, in what looked to Benjamin like the most curious pose he'd seen so far. Queen Dearie obviously didn't think so. She clapped her paws delightedly as she told Cringe and Simper, 'Look-you! Remembers-she how-to smiley-beg!'

Mops was sitting cross-legged. Her spine was straight. Her arms were tucked in to her sides, her hands cupped together to form the shape of a food bowl. And, as if this wasn't enough, Mops had arranged her face into the biggest smile she could manage.

'What are you *doing*?' shouted Benjamin angrily.

'I'm doing what she wants me to do,' answered Mops, still smiling.

'Well, I'm not,' retorted Benjamin angrily.

Queen Dearie had turned her attention onto him. Her sharp brown eyes had lost the soft glow they'd had when she was looking at Mops. Now they were glittering and determined.

'Smiley-beg,' she told Benjamin. Mops was still in position, so the Queen pointed a claw at her and repeated the word. 'Smiley-beg'.

Benjamin felt a rage bubbling up inside him. The terrible news about his mother, the despair of knowing that his father was still chained up on the Galley-Royal, and now being expected to perform this ridiculous trick for this stupid queen-bear...added together it was becoming almost unbearable. He took a deep breath to try and control his temper...

Then Cringe and Simper descended on him from either side. As Simper grabbed Benjamin and sat him down, Cringe took a firm grip on his hands and tried to force them into a cup shape. And while this was going on, Queen Dearie was getting nearer and nearer to him, growling repeatedly, 'Smiley-beg, smiley-beg...' until her wet, brown snout was right in front of him.

So Benjamin punched it. Hard.

Wrestling his right arm free from Cringe's grip, he let loose all his bubbling fury in a blow which landed smack in the middle of Queen Dearie's snout with a *very* satisfying thump.

Queen Dearie's howl of pained surprise was instantly followed by an enraged bellow: 'Treason! For-that will-you head-lose!'

Benjamin didn't hesitate. With a wild wriggle and a flailing of fists he broke free from the clutches of Simper and Cringe and raced away. His only thought was to get back to the Galley-Royal and to his father, despite the danger that might bring.

Speeding across the grass, he headed for the nearest entrance to the Palace. Once he was inside he'd surely be able to shake off his pursuers in its maze of corridors and turnings. Swerving past an ornate scratching post topped with a golden crown, Benjamin saw the way to go. An entrance was ahead. It lay at the end of a petal-strewn pathway and was garlanded with flowers and berries. If he'd had time to think, Benjamin might have suspected that it was a special entrance, perhaps reserved for the king and queen. But he didn't – and so hurtled straight into a King Antonius still angry about what Benjamin had seen (though not yet understood) happening in that dreadful pit.

'You-got!' snarled the king, grabbing Benjamin and holding him fast until Simper and Cringe rumbled up and he could hand him over. This time the two flunky-bears gripped Benjamin so hard that little drops of blood oozed out from where their claws were sticking into his skin. Together with King Antonius they took him back to where Queen Dearie was sitting, still rubbing her tender snout.

'Sap-that,' she demanded of the king, 'Must head-lose!'

King Antonius shrugged. 'If wish-you, love-my,' he said, his mind quite clearly on other things. 'For-what?'

'He snout-me-punched!' roared the queen.

'Really?' said the king. His tone of voice had changed from irritated to intrigued. He was looking at the furious Benjamin with a new interest. 'One-small him-like?'

Queen Dearie stamped a heavy foot. 'Cares-who if one-small? He hard-me-punched! Now executioner-take!'

'No!' screamed Mops who, until now, had been looking on in a terrified silence. As Cringe and Simper began to drag Benjamin back towards the palace, she scurried to the queen's side and buried her face in the she-bear's furry stomach. 'Please don't!'

King Antonius's face broke into a sly smile. Though he – like the queen – hadn't understood Mops's screeching, its meaning had seemed very clear. 'Thinks-she hurt-you-will her sap-friend.'

'Head-slice hurts-not,' snapped Queen Dearie, 'It over-all in blink-eye. She swish-quick, then rolling-gone.'

Another wail from Mops gave the king the opening he'd been looking for. Refusing to do what Queen Dearie wanted was never easy, not unless she could be persuaded to want something else even more. Now, stroking his chin, he said to his wife, 'Have-me idea-better.'

'Hah!' scoffed the queen. 'Possible-not!'

'No?' said King Antonius, giving the still-struggling Benjamin another look of approval, 'About-how…'

As the king began to outline his thinking, Queen Dearie's face slowly changed. Her look of thunder cleared. A smile began to form and grow. By the time King Antonius had finished whispering, she was growl-chuckling with pleasure.

'That *is* idea-better,' she said. 'Pain-extra-full! Agree-me!'

Moving Mops gently to one side, she called loudly to Cringe and Simper to drag Benjamin back into her royal presence once more. By the time he arrived, the flunky-bears' claws had dug even deeper into his skin.

112

Blood was now trickling down his arm. The queen looked at it and beamed.

'More-much blood-lose where going-you,' she purred. 'Away-him-take!'

'Yes, Majesty-your,' said Cringe.

'Once-at, Majesty-your,' said Simper, before asking, 'Er…to-where?'

King Antonius answered. 'Where think-you? To the lonely-den!'

He gave Benjamin a final look of approval. A sap wild enough and brave enough to punch the Queen Dearie on the snout – something that he himself had never been able to summon up the courage to do! How could he allow such a sap to be executed, especially when he'd just sent his current sap away to be sold after his pitiful showing in the pit? A sap like this was worth his weight in gold. Worth *more* than his weight in gold.

Telling Queen Dearie that this sap was going to suffer greatly had been a master stroke. The hair-red would suffer, no doubt about it. But not, if he was any judge, all at once. It would take some time for him to be killed. And before that time came this sap was going to win him, King Antonius, an awful lot of money.

Oh, yes.

For an awful lot of money was just what you could win if you were the owner of a top fighting-sap.

THE FIGHTING-PIT

The lonely-den was well named. It was a cramped, round chamber deep beneath the walls of Bearkingdom-Palace. The only way into this chamber was through its solid wooden door. This door had a small, barred grille set into its top section. And that was it. The lonely-den had no window for the sun to shine through, no bench for Benjamin to sit or lie down on, no straw for a bed, no food or drink bowls – nothing. All Benjamin could do was sit on the cold, hard floor...and wait.

The only visitor he had was a tough, gnarled keeper-bear with ears shaped like a couple of flower-caulis. He turned up now and again to throw a chain round Benjamin's neck and take him out into a tiny open-air courtyard to do his business. While there Benjamin was allowed to take a drink from a bucket of water, but that was all. He hasn't been given a scrap of food to eat. Nor had so much as a bite been pushed through the grille or under the door. By the time three sun-comes had passed, hunger was gnawing horribly at his insides.

So when, through the door grille, he saw the black snout and beady eyes of no less a visitor than King Antonius himself, Benjamin couldn't stop himself yelling, 'I'm starving! Give me some food! Please!'

He knew the king couldn't understand what he was shouting, so he accompanied his yells with signs and movements that even the slowest-brained bear couldn't mistake. Benjamin opened his mouth wide and pointed. He held his stomach and groaned. Finally, he cast aside every shred of pride that he had and held out his cupped hands in the smiley-beg position.

Seeing this, King Antonius growl-chuckled. He gave a satisfied nod. He said, 'Good-very.' Then he padded away.

Another sun-come passed before the king returned. This time Benjamin screamed even louder, getting into the smiley-beg position at once.

'Please give me something to eat! I beg you! I'm so hungry!'

King Antonius looked even more pleased this time. 'Ready-soon, thinks-me,' he said mysteriously.

Benjamin had no idea what the king could mean and he didn't care. All he cared about now was getting something to eat. If there had been straw on the floor he'd have devoured it all, he was that hungry. So when the king's snout appeared at the fighter-den grille after yet another foodless sun-come had passed, Benjamin didn't beg.

'Food!' he screamed wildly. 'Food! I must have food!'

He didn't even try the smiley-beg position. Instead, in his desperate desire to make the king understand, Benjamin launched himself frantically at the door. When it merely shuddered, he lost all control. Screaming at the top of his voice, Benjamin ran round and round the tiny den until finally he slumped to the floor and cried his heart out.

At this, King Antonius smiled broadly. 'Aha! Ready-definite,' he said, and added, 'Testing-time, thinks-me.'

The king returned soon after. This time he wasn't alone. Neither was he empty-pawed.

With him was the burly keeper-bear who until now had only taken him out for business-doing and water-drinking. The moment his door swung open this keeper-bear rushed in to grab Benjamin and hold him still.

'Him-me-got, Majesty-your!'

Assured that he wouldn't be attacked, King Antonius entered the fighter-den. Benjamin now saw what the king had brought with him.

First, a pair of bear's fore-paws. Not real ones, still attached to a bear, but as real as could be. They were black, furry – and, in particular, held a full set of razor-sharp claws. The only unreal thing about them was that these fore-paws weren't filled with muscles and

116

bones: they were hollow. Benjamin was still wondering what they were for when, with the speed which comes of practice, King Antonius quickly slid the forepaws over Benjamin's hands and tied them tightly at the wrist.

Within moments to these were added a pair of rear paws. They were as black, furry and sharp-clawed as the pair of fore-paws, except that these were pulled up over Benjamin's feet and tied firmly round his legs.

Benjamin gasped. A memory, brief and horrific, came to him and it was all he could do to stop himself crying out in fear. For the memory had revealed to him what was coming next. A mask.

A mask in the shape of a bear's head. It had a high, furry brow. It had a long snout. It had teeth which matched the claws for sharpness. The keeper-bear now held Benjamin's neck still so that King Antonius could lower this head over Benjamin's own head.

Now Benjamin *did* cry out. He gave a cry of pain and confusion and terror, all rolled into one. A cry such he'd heard only once before – when he'd stumbled across the strange pit and seen that awful creature in it. For that was the memory that had come to him. In that moment he'd realised to his horror that the creature hadn't been half-bear, half-human at all. It had simply been a boy, forced to wear a bear's claws and head. And now that boy had been replaced by him.

'Looks-him-good!' said King Antonius, stepping

back and studying Benjamin. 'Think-you-not?'

'Definitely, Majesty-your!' answered the keeper-bear.

'But will-him fight-good?' wondered the King.

'The fighting-pit is ready-all, Majesty-your,' said the keeper-bear.

King Antonius smiled grimly. 'Then test-me my fighting-sap!'

Hearing this, Benjamin's heart pounded even faster than it already was. He was going to be taken to that pit. He was going to have to fight – or else. A wave of fear surged through his whole body.

Feeling as though his legs would give way at any moment, the masked and clawed Benjamin was led out of the den and along a damp-walled passageway. In spite of his fear, he immediately realised how carefully the bear mask had been designed. Its eye-holes were large enough for him to see where he was going. Through its small ears he could hear the sounds of his clawed feet scratching along the cobbled ground.

He was heading towards a tall, barred gate behind which a dim light shone. Reaching it, the keeper-bear paused and looked at King Antonius. The king nodded. The keeper-bear pulled a dangling chain. Immediately the torch-lights behind the gate flared brightly. Benjamin gasped as he saw the dusty-floored pit he'd seen from above on the day he met Rosetta Willowthin – the pit in which he'd seen the boy he'd mistaken for a nightmare creature. The same boy who was waiting for him now...

'Sap,' growled King Antonius as the gate was flung open and Benjamin was pushed through by the keeper-bear, 'fight-you!'

The boy had his back to Benjamin. He was crouching down in the very centre of the pit. Benjamin edged forward. The boy didn't turn, not even when the barred gate clanged – and, for his part, Benjamin didn't call out. Quietly, he crept closer.

He was no longer trembling. His fear had gone. The boy was guarding a food bowl. Benjamin had caught the mouth-watering smells of wild berries and tasty sweetmeats the moment he'd been thrust into the fighting-pit. And in that instant his terror had been swamped by the overwhelming desire to satisfy his hunger. This boy had food. He, Benjamin, wanted that food. He *needed* it. And nothing was going to stop him having it...

With a terrible howl, Benjamin lunged forward. Flinging his claw-tipped arms round the boy's neck he tried to throw him aside. But the boy stayed firm. Benjamin dug his claws into the boy's garments, neither thinking nor caring about them cutting through to the skin beneath. He tried to lift and throw the boy in one movement, only to find that he was surprisingly heavy. Driven mad by the thoughts of the food within his reach, Benjamin now lost all control. Finding extra strength from somewhere, he howled and hit and pulled and slashed and dragged until finally the boy toppled aside.

Without even thinking about what condition he'd left the boy in, Benjamin fell on the food, scooping it up in handfuls and stuffing it beneath the bear mask and into his mouth. All too soon it was gone. Benjamin did the only thing left to him. He lifted the bowl to his lips, licking and scouring until all he could taste was the clay the bowl had been made from.

Only then did Benjamin think about the other boy – and realise that not once had he tried to fight back and land a blow of his own. He hadn't resisted at all, just sat there and allowed Benjamin to claw wildly at him. Lifting his head, Benjamin looked for the first time at what was left of his opponent.

The 'boy' was lying on his side, motionless. His garments were in shreds. Straw poked out in tufts through the gaps in his chest. And, now visible through the gash Benjamin had clawed in his side, was the large rock that had made him seem so heavy. He'd fought and defeated a dummy! Benjamin didn't know whether to laugh or cry.

The burly keeper-bear came in then. Hauling Benjamin to his feet, he dragged him back to the lonely-den. The claws and his bear's mask had just been taken off when King Antonius arrived. He was gloating.

'Full-wonder! Hair-red-this is fighting-sap-ferocious!'

'And against-only a sap-pretend, Majesty-your,' said the keeper-bear.

'True-too!' The king rubbed his paws in delight. 'Money-me-win plenty-pots when same-he-does to opponent-real!'

After they'd left him, Benjamin sat in the dark. He thought of how hungry he still was, and of how much hungrier he was going to get – for apart from what he'd gulped down in the fighting-pit they'd given him nothing else to eat. And then the final few gloating words of King Antonius would ring in his head, '...*when same-he-does to opponent-real!*'

That's what he was there for. That's why he wasn't being fed. Some time soon King Antonius was going to make him fight over a bowl of food with a real boy, so that he and his friends – the bearons, almost certainly – could lay bets on who would win. King Antonius clearly expected it to be him. By starving Benjamin he was fully expecting that by the time the fight took place he would be so hungry that he would rip apart any opponent who stood between him and some food.

A great shudder passed through Benjamin's whole body. For he knew in his heart that the king was right.

MOPS'S DECISION

Mops was feeling terrible too.

She was fearful about what might be happening to Benjamin. She was also fearful about what might be happening to her.

Benjamin's angry question in the garden had struck home. Was she enjoying herself in Bearkingdom-Palace too much to want to run away? She simply didn't know. She'd once been a sap-pet and it had been so boring! But after the horrors of the Howling-Tower and the Galley-Royal, being pampered and cared for again *was* nice. Being told she was special *was* nice. But having wonderful friends like Benjamin Wildfire – and stupid, brave, miserable Spike Brownberry who she'd last seen running away from the Howling-Tower – was *far* nicer.

Now Spike was gone and she didn't know what had become of poor Benjamin. Mops, lolling at Queen Dearie's feet on a velvet cushion, suddenly felt more alone than she'd ever felt before. What was she to do?

It was then that King Antonius swept in. So pleased was he with the performance of his new fighting-sap that he'd hurried straight to tell his wife all about him.

'The hair-red ferocious-is!' he crowed. 'Beat-him-will comers-all at the Banquet-Royal! Bet-you!'

'Said-you-that time-last!' growl-snapped Queen Dearie, who loved spending money but hated losing it. 'And happened-what? Lost-you-me my precious hair-red never-move to Bearon Weimar!'

At the queen's feet, Mops dipped her writing nail in her pot of ink-blue and continued to practise her words. But she was all ears.

'Yes, yes, know-me,' sighed King Antonius, who'd lost count of how many times he'd been reminded of the lost never-move. 'But sap-this can back-her-win!'

Queen Dearie's eyes narrowed in suspicion. 'Said-you the snout-puncher suffer-would,' she growled. 'Pain-extra-full, said-you.'

The King patted her gently on the forearm. 'And will-it so-be,' he said softly. 'Hear-me the fighting-sap of Bearon Weimar is bruiser-big. Expect-me the hair-red to him-beat only after spill-blood-much.'

'The snout-puncher is fighting-good, then?'

'Very,' nodded the king.

'Fighting-mean? Fighting-hungry?'

'Mean-very,' King Antonius assured her. 'Has-never a fighting-sap hungrier-been!'

'Really?' Queen Dearie, still not completely convinced, lumbered to her feet. 'This,' she said, 'must-me-see.'

And so, with Mops trailing dutifully at her side, Queen Dearie followed King Antonius along the Bearkingdom-Palace corridors, down echoing steps, and through grim passageways until finally they stopped at the lonely-den door. The burly keeper-bear lounging outside snapped to attention, then made himself scarce.

At the sight of the king's face behind the grille in his door, Benjamin screamed for all he was worth, 'Give me something to eat!' he raged.

When the inquisitive face of Queen Dearie replaced the king's, Benjamin's fury boiled over. Oh, how he wanted to punch that big, wet snout again! How he wanted to make her pay for having him put in this cramped and filthy chamber! Howling madly, Benjamin charged across the chill, cobbled floor of the den and hurled himself at the door.

Queen Dearie retreated hurriedly. 'See-me what mean-you,' she said, impressed. 'Never-me-known one fighting-hungry-so!'

King Antonius gave her a so-told-you look. 'And still-be sun-comes-three until Banquet-Royal. Will-he be food-ravenous by then!'

Another three sun-comes before he'd see food?

Hearing this, Benjamin jumped furiously at the door again. This time he looped his fingers in the rusting metal grille and clawed his way up until he could look through. That was when he saw Mops, standing obediently beside Queen Dearie.

'Mops!' yelled Benjamin.

Then his strength failed him. Unable to cling on any longer, he fell to the floor. He carried on shouting, though, simply wanting to hear Mops's voice again.

'Mops!' he called. 'Are you still there?'

There was a pause. Then, joy of joys, Mops called in reply.

'Yes, I'm here. The king's just taken Queen Dearie off to show her the fighting-pit, whatever that is.' Benjamin heard her stifle a cry. 'Oh Benjamin, why couldn't you have just smiley-begged like the queen wanted?'

'Don't start that again, Mops,' shouted Benjamin.

'But you look so *awful*! And here's me looking pretty and getting writing lessons and everything. I've got my own scratch-pad now, you know.'

'Mops...' said Benjamin urgently. He'd just had a thought.

'I'm getting on ever so well. I can write lots of words! "Good" and "Bad"; "Hello" and "Bye-good"; "King" and "Queen"...'

'Mops!'

'"Queen" is really tricky. Then there's "Food" and "drink"...'

The mention of these last two words sent Benjamin scrambling up to the grille again.

'Mops!' he pleaded, 'I'm starving! Can you get me some food?'

Mops looked up with tears in her eyes. 'You've got a fight coming up. At the Banquet-Royal.'

'What?'

'King Antonius told Queen Dearie all about it. You'll be against Bearon Weimar's fighting-sap. The king's hoping you'll win him lots of money...'

'Mops, answer the question! Will you get me some food?'

'...To make up for him losing your mother to Bearon Weimar!' Mops screamed.

Benjamin gazed down at her in stunned silence. When he did try to speak, his tongue felt as if was tied in knots. Finally he managed, 'Lost her?'

'Yes! In a bet! She must still be there, at Bearon Weimar's place!'

Shafts of hope flooded into Benjamin's heart – together with a renewed determination to get away. So far it had been impossible. The keeper-bear had only ever let him out to do his business in the high-walled courtyard. But perhaps if he won this fight they'd treat him more kindly...take him out to the garden...give him a chance to run...

'I've got to win, Mops!' he shouted, gritting his teeth

with the effort of clinging to the grille. 'I've got to win this fight!'

'I do hope so, Benjamin,' cried Mops. 'I'll be thinking of you!'

'I don't want you to think of me! I want you to get me some food!'

'I can't,' said Mops quietly.

'You can!' snapped Benjamin angrily. 'All you have to do is hide away some of those treats you're getting for all that wonderful writing!'

Mops smiled weakly. 'Queen Dearie's talking about showing me off at the Banquet-Royal...'

'Just hide some treats, some of your dinner, anything,' yelled Benjamin, 'and get it to me!'

From the end of the corridor came an annoyed roar. The king and queen had finished inspecting the fighting-pit and the burly keeper-bear, escorting them back again, had just spotted Benjamin up at the grille. There was no time to lose.

'Please, Mops! Will you try to get me some food!'

Mops looked up at him. Her eyes welled up with tears and she felt so sad that she could hardly speak. But finally she managed to say it, 'No, Benjamin. I can't.'

Benjamin let go of the grille and slumped to the lonely-den floor. From outside came the sounds of heavy paw-steps and dainty footsteps moving away. He buried his face in his hands.

Then he wept silent tears of mourning for the death

of his friendship with Millicent Ophelia Patience Snubnose (Mops for short).

Back in the queen's chambers, Mops buried her face in a velvet cushion. She hadn't meant to babble on about her writing and everything, but she'd been so unhappy.

From what the king had said about starving Benjamin she'd just known that he would ask her to get him some food. And she'd also known that, hard as it would be, she would have to refuse.

Now she was frightened – so, so frightened – that he would meet his end without understanding why.

And she wept tears of hope for the safety of her dearest friend, Benjamin Wildfire.

MAY-WIN THE SAP-BEST!

Three sun-comes later, Benjamin awoke knowing that this was *the day*.

He didn't know this because he'd counted the sun-comes since Mops had refused to help him. Benjamin hadn't seen the sun. It didn't penetrate into the gloomy courtyard he was taken to for business and drinking. For all he knew it could be dawn-crack or middle-night while he was there.

Neither did Benjamin suspect it was *the day* because of the hustle and bustle going on in the Palace. He didn't see the army of flunkies decorating it from top to bottom, strewing extra-fragrant blooms over every floor and draping sweet-smelling honeysuckle over every wall, while a critical Queen Dearie watched their every move. Nor did he hear any of the blow-horn fanfares which sounded as middle-day approached and the stream of invited guests began to arrive for the Banquet-Royal.

No, what told Benjamin that this was *the day* was awaking to see King Antonius peering through the grille in the door. Since bringing Queen Dearie to see him the king had been visiting more and more often, but never had he brought any food with him. This time he had. Benjamin, who thought he'd been dreaming that a delicious-smelling, juice-oozing morsel of food had been dangled through the grille suddenly realised that that's exactly what was happening.

With a roar of delight, Benjamin threw himself across the den – only to find the dripping morsel yanked sharply away from him before he could grab it. His delight turned to a door-thumping rage. Outside, King Antonius growl-laughed in satisfaction.

Not long after, he was back again. Once more the juicy morsel was dangled temptingly down. Again, Benjamin's jump was too late. The next time, Benjamin tried crouching beneath the grille, ready to try and snatch the food away the moment it came through. But the king realised he was there and this time poor Benjamin did worse than fail. As the morsel was whipped away, he managed to get the merest touch. The mouth-watering smell left on Benjamin's fingertips after the king had padded off almost drove him mad.

Now, as he heard paw-steps outside once more, he readied himself. A wild fury bubbled through every bone of his body. He was going to hammer at the door, bend the iron bars of the grille – whatever it took – or perish in the attempt.

The paw-steps halted. But this time no food was

pushed tantalisingly through the grille. Instead, the door swung open. In rushed the burly keeper-bear, ready to grab him and hold him tight. There was no need. For Benjamin knew what this meant. King Antonius had been deliberately driving him wild because it was *the day*. And now it was *the time*.

So Benjamin didn't kick and scream. When King Antonius came in carrying the fighting claws and bear mask and pulled them over his hands, feet and head, he didn't buck or struggle. When the king led the way out of the fighter-den, Benjamin didn't try to dig his feet-claws into the floor to try and stop them.

No. Deep down, he was pleased. It was time – and he was ready. In that fighting-pit there would be food waiting to be won. The thought of it sent waves of power rippling through his body. Yes, he was ready – and he pitied the poor sap-fighter chosen to stand in his way. He was going to have to hurt him. In his heart he knew he should feel sorry about that, but he didn't. After all, wasn't his opponent going to try and do the same to him? King Antonius's treatment had worked. It had turned him into an animal, just like the bears.

They'd reached the barred gate leading into the fighting-pit. Before, when they'd tested him against the dummy-sap, King Antonius had stayed outside. Not this time. Swinging the gate open with a flourish, the king marched straight on into the fighting-pit. He was greeted by a bloodthirsty growl-roar of anticipation.

Benjamin looked up. The high, passage-like gallery which encircled the fighting-pit was packed. Rows of excited bears were jammed tightly together, those at the front almost leaning over the edge of the pit so as to get the best view. Drips of eager slobber were trickling from their mouths and running down the fighting-pit's steep, round wall towards the thick dust of its floor.

King Antonius raised a paw for silence. 'Begin-now the Banquet-Royal fight-big!' he announced with a flourish. 'Here-be fighter-mine!'

Benjamin was now led into the fighting-pit by his keeper-bear. Immediately, another growl-roar erupted – a growl-roar just like the one he'd heard when Roger Broadback was being tormented in the sap-garden. It was the growl-roar of excitedly shouted bets.

'Rounds-fifty king's-sap to fight-win!' hollered an unseen bear.

'Rounds-ten draws-he blood-first!' bawled another.

This went on for a few moments until it was swamped by another growl-roar of welcome. A bear wearing a huge chain of office was pushing through the barred gate to join King Antonius in the centre of the fighting-pit: Bearon Weimar.

'And here-be,' announced the bearon confidently, 'fighter-mine!'

The bearon was a striking figure. His fur was tinged a silvery grey, except for that around his muzzle which was an almost pure white. In contrast, his nine claws were a jet black – nine, because the middle one on his right paw was missing. As he now pointed towards the fighting-pit gate with this paw, the baying audience fell briefly silent. Then, as Benjamin's opponent was brought in, uproar broke out again.

'Rounds-ten says quick-he-wins!'

'Rounds-fifty Weimar-sap ear-rips!'

'Rounds-hundred bet-me king's-sap slaughtered-is!'

In spite of the coldness in Benjamin's heart, a tremble of fear swept through his body. His opponent was, like him, fitted out with a bear's mask and two sets of claws. But his mask looked fiercer than Benjamin's. His claws looked bigger than Benjamin's. As for the boy beneath, he was bigger than Benjamin too. His legs were longer, his arms were stronger, his chest more powerful. Worst of all, he seemed even hungrier. He was being held back by not one, but *two* keeper-bears.

Into the uproar a new bet was now shouted, loudly and clearly. It came from Bearon Weimar.

'Bet-me thousand-fifty on fighter-mine!'

A shocked hush fell over the gallery. A bet of a fifty thousand rounds was huge. But into the silence King Antonius shouted: 'Accept-me – and raise-me! Bet-me thousand-*hundred* on fighter-*mine*!'

Hearing this, Bearon Weimar scratched his white muzzle thoughtfully. Slowly he shook his head. 'Not-can afford-me thousand-hundred,' he said, only to add with an ugly smirk, 'but sure-you-am, Majesty-your? Not-remember Banquet-last…when lose-you the never-move?'

Now the voice of Queen Dearie cut through the growing babble. 'Remember-we right-all! So how-say-we our thousand-hundred against your thousand-fifty…*and* the hair-red never-move won-you time-last!'

'Done!' growl-shouted Bearon Weimar immediately. 'Bet-me thousand-fifty and the Alicia-sap!'

Alicia! At the sound of his mother's name Benjamin's heart turned a somersault. Mops had been right. This *was* the Bearon who'd taken her away! It was almost more than he'd dared to hope. She was alive and well. What was more, the bearon's bet against the king and queen meant that if he won the fight, she would be on her way back to Bearkingdom-Palace!

If he won the fight…

Benjamin's elation gave way to anxiety. While the betting had been going on, Bearon Weimar's terrifyingly big fighting-sap had grown to look even more dangerous. He was now kicking and struggling so much that his sweating keeper-bears had difficulty in holding on to him. Benjamin now realised why. It was because his opponent had seen something that he hadn't.

Dangling high above the fighting-pit was a giant bowl. It was brimming with berries and sweetmeats and

134

fruits and honey-drenched nut-doughs and a lot more besides. Slowly, this bowl had begun to descend.

As it came lower, Benjamin's opponent struggled all the more. He gave a howl of desire. Then another howl split the air – and Benjamin realised that it had come not from the other boy, but from himself. He too was straining to get away from his burly keeper-bear and get to the bowl. The sight of it…and, oh, the smells now drifting down from it, were beginning to drive him wild.

The bowl stopped, suspended above the centre of the pit. Benjamin desperately tried to calm himself. He had to think clearly. If he rushed headlong towards that bowl, his bigger and stronger opponent would tear him apart. He had to be clever…

King Antonius was clutching paws with Bearon Weimar. 'Hope-me for fight-good,' he lied, not caring whether it was good or not so long as he won.

'May-win sap-best!' replied Bearon Weimar confidently, clearly expecting that sap to be his own.

These false promises over, the two bears quickly left by the fighting-pit gate. But still Benjamin and his opponent weren't released. Only when King Antonius and Bearon Weimar reappeared up in the gallery, taking their places in the front row, did that happen.

Slowly, King Antonius lifted his right paw – then swiftly brought it down again with a cutting motion. On this signal, Benjamin's keeper-bear released him and dived out through the gate. At the same instant, his powerful opponent's two keepers did the same. A great roar of anticipation rose from the gallery.

And so the sap-fight began...

THE SAP-FIGHT

With a blood-curdling shout, Benjamin's opponent immediately charged across the dusty floor of the fighting-pit.

Benjamin charged too. But, while his opponent wildly jumped straight for the dangling bowl of food, Benjamin didn't. Instead, he carried on running – to crash straight into the other boy's legs and send him toppling to the ground with a howl of surprise and a mighty thump. Almost at once, though, the boy had struggled back onto his knees. But still his eyes were fixed on the bowl above their heads. Benjamin had a plan, and he didn't hesitate. Launching himself fiercely into the boy's chest, he knocked him flat on his back so that his bear-masked head thumped against the fighting-pit floor.

Benjamin's opponent lay stunned and groaning. He was shaking his head back and forth as if he was trying to clear it, but was clearly too dazed to get back on his feet. *Now* Benjamin could concentrate on the food bowl. He scurried backwards, almost to the sheer round wall of the fighting-pit. Then he raced forward. As he got closer to the food bowl he stretched out his false-clawed arm. Then, just a pace away, he leapt and reached and stretched with all his might...and came down with nothing.

At the crucial moment the bowl had been jerked upwards and out of his reach. From the gallery came a burst of growl-laughing.

'Food-none till blood-spill!' roared a drooling, wild-eyed spectator-bear.

So that was it, realised Benjamin. There was no escape. To win this contest it wasn't going to be enough for him to grab the food first. The baying bears expected him to hurt his opponent as well. They wouldn't be satisfied until they'd seen some blood. And Benjamin didn't doubt that they knew just how to make it happen. For even as the other boy began to stir himself, the bowl was being lowered again. By the time Benjamin's opponent had struggled on to all fours, the bowl had stopped in the worst spot possible: high enough to be just out of reach even with the mightiest leap...but low enough for them to catch the full delicious aroma of the gorgeous food it held.

Benjamin felt his heart swelling with desire. Without even realising he was doing it, he spread his hands wide to extend the fearsome claws they'd been clad in. If he had to tear and rip then he would...

He turned back to his opponent. But before he could

make a move, Benjamin was caught by surprise. Without bothering to get to his feet, the other boy launched himself forward. Benjamin cried out with pain as a sharp claw dug into his leg and he was now himself brought crashing down into the clinging dust of the fighting-pit floor. Claws raised viciously, the other boy was about to dive on top of him. Benjamin rolled to one side in the nick of time, leaving his powerful opponent to land beside him with a thump.

Benjamin sprang to his feet. His opponent may have been bigger, but he was also slower. He was still struggling to get up, the claws on his hands and feet gouging grooves in the dirt as he did so. It was Benjamin's chance, and he took it. Leaping on to the boy's back, he pushed down as hard as he possibly could. The boy tensed, trying to resist Benjamin's weight – then, like a collapsing bridge, suddenly fell flat on his stomach. Benjamin pinned him to the ground with his knees. Roaring madly, the boy bucked and jerked but hunger and the smell of the food had given Benjamin a strength he didn't know he had. Try as he might, the other boy couldn't throw him off. Slowly he weakened. Benjamin felt as if an icy hand had gripped his heart. The blood-thirsty bears were going to get their wish. He was going to do what he had to do. He was going to finish this fight, here and now.

As his opponent's head sank to the dust, Benjamin moved both hands round the boy's neck. For a moment he held them there, his razor-sharp claws poised just above the boy's skin. He'd won – and was suddenly afraid of what that meant. He knew that all he had to do now was dig and rip...

Benjamin's beaten opponent knew it, too. Beneath him the boy's powerful frame had gone soft with resignation.

'You win,' he heard him groan. 'Get it over and done with, matey.'

Matey?

That single word cut through to Benjamin's cold heart like a firebrand through snow. Only one person he'd ever known had called people 'matey': a brave boy he'd been proud to call a friend; a boy he'd last seen in the dreaded Howling-Tower.

'Spike?' he cried. 'Is that you?'

From beneath the boy's bear mask came a gasp of astonishment. 'Yeah. Yeah, it is...'

'It's me! Benjamin!'

'Benjamin? Benjamin Wildfire?'

'Yes!'

'Well this is *me*! Spike Brownberry!'

The instant Benjamin had gripped Spike's neck with his claws, an expectant hush had fallen over the gallery. The two boys' hurried conversation since then had been taken as sap-squeakings of fear and anger. This was normal. Sap-squeakings added to the juiciness of the event. A nice, prolonged kill was *so* much

140

more enjoyable than a quick slash-wallop. But sap-squeakings could go on for too long – and these had, especially for King Antonius. The bear king was already counting his winnings.

'Off-him-finish!' he roared at Benjamin.

Sitting nearby, and worried that he'd have no winnings to count, Bearon Weimar now bellowed at Spike: 'Back-fight!'.

For a moment these shouts filled Benjamin with dread – but only for a moment. Almost as quickly an idea began to form. He bent low, so that Spike could hear him over the hubbub. 'Spike! We've got to carry on fighting!'

'No, Benjamin,' answered Spike. 'I'd rather let Bearon Weimar sell me to the bone-merchants than fight you.'

'But we're not going to fight *properly*, Spike. We're going to *pretend*!'

'Pretend?' echoed Spike. 'That's different. Get ready, matey!'

And so, to the great delight of the watching bears, Spike quickly jerked his back upwards as if he'd recovered enough strength to try and throw Benjamin off. As for Benjamin, he played his part by dramatically crashing to one side as if he'd been caught by surprise.

Spike rolled over, and up on to his feet. He lashed out at Benjamin's arm with his sharp claws, but made sure he missed. Benjamin gave the opposite impression to the spectator-bears, though, screaming in agony and clutching his arm as if Spike really had gouged a lump out of it. He reeled backwards for good measure – and was rewarded by a stroke of good fortune.

Worried that Bearon Weimer's sap was recovering, King Antonius had decided to give Benjamin an extra boost by signalling for the brimming bowl of food to be lowered again. Down it came, only for Benjamin to clatter into it as he reeled backwards. The bowl swung wildly in a circle. It began to rise, out of reach – only for Spike, pretending to be closing in on Benjamin, to loop out his longest claw and drag it to the floor of the fighting-pit. Glorious, wonderful food spilled out everywhere.

'Grab some, quick!' shouted Spike, diving for a handful of nuts.

Benjamin snatched up a particularly juicy red fruit. 'Not all at once,' he shouted at Spike. 'We've got to keep fighting as well!'

That much was very clear. The renewed action had set the bears roaring with delight. But they wanted something more than a fight. Rolling down from the gallery came an evil chant.

'Want-we blood-spill! Want-we blood-spill!'

Spike was still busily stuffing nuts into his mouth. Benjamin took a bite out of the red fruit, then continued to stagger round holding his 'seriously injured' arm until Spike was finished. Then, with what he hoped sounded like a howl of anger, he launched

142

across to Spike and grabbed him round the waist.

'Go backwards!' he hissed.

With Spike pretending to be unable to prevent him, Benjamin ran them both across the fighting-pit floor and up against its wall. Only then did he let the remainder of the red fruit slip out from its hiding place in the palm of his clawed hand – and, in spite of the almost overwhelming desire to stuff it into his mouth, did something else with it instead. He squashed it down between their chests.

'Aaaargh!' he screamed loudly, reeling backwards.

'Ooh!' moaned Spike, slumping dramatically to his knees.

'Blood-spill! Blood-spill!' roared the spectators, seeing the deep red stains spreading across each boy's shirt.

Benjamin now lunged, wobbly-legged, for the food bowl. Spike gave him enough time to gulp down a gloriously tasty nut-dough. Then he charged across and thumped Benjamin sideways with a blow that looked powerful but felt as light as a feather.

And so it went on.

With lots of realistic groaning and yelling and staggering and falling and head-holding, Benjamin and Spike completely fooled the watching bears, whilst at the same time taking it in turns to eat almost everything the food bowl held. The only things that didn't go into their mouths were the things like squashy tomatoes and juicy beetroots which they secretly squashed against each other to make the blood-thirsty spectators think they really were tearing each other to shreds.

But there was one other thing they did as they 'fought': they planned. Somehow, they had to bring this battle to an end. Benjamin gasped out his idea for how to do it. Spike groaned as he agreed that it was a good one. With a groan of his own, Benjamin said, 'Let's try it, then!'

And so on they went, pretend-fighting until finally there was just one thing left in the food bowl – the sweetest, most mouth-watering pineapple that either of them had ever smelled. By then, both Spike and Benjamin were on their knees, trying to look as though they were exhausted. Up in the gallery, King Antonius and Queen Dearie leaned forward, flecks of spit sailing out of their wet mouths as they roared.

'Pineapple-grab, hair-red! Pineapple-grab!'

A pop-eyed Bearon Weimar was bawling the same thing at Spike. 'It-get, bruiser-big!'

So that was the rule – the winner of these terrible contests was the fighting-sap who took the last thing from the bowl. Benjamin gasped as much to Spike.

'Ready?' he hissed. Spike nodded.

Benjamin began to edge clumsily forward, making it look as if he was totally exhausted. From the other side of the food bowl, Spike did the same. He thrust out a red-stained arm. Benjamin slumped to his knees before he, too, jabbed out a hand. And so, just as planned, the two friends both sank their false claws into the pineapple at exactly the same moment...and collapsed.

The gallery erupted in an explosion of noise, with most of the spectator-bears agreeing that it had been the best, the bloodiest, sap-fight they'd seen for many a moon. Only King Antonius and Bearon Weimar seemed upset.

'A match-drawn,' growled the king. 'Agree-you?'

'Agree-me,' said Bearon Weimar sourly.

King Antonius turned to Queen Dearie and shrugged. 'On-look the side-bright,' he said. 'Lost-we-not.'

'And won-we-not,' she snapped. 'So return-not my never-move!' Pointing an imperious claw down at Benjamin and Spike, both still motionless of the floor of the fighting-pit, the queen bellowed at the keeper-bears waiting outside the fighting-pit's gate. 'Away-them-drag!'

Benjamin's heart gave a flip. This was it, their big chance. Pretend-fighting to a draw had only been part of the plan that he and Spike had worked out. There was more, but it was risky. It all depended on the keeper-bears. If they simply dragged him and Spike away, then it wouldn't work. He had to do something to prevent that happening.

Out of the corner of his eye, Benjamin saw his own burly keeper-bear come through the fighting-pit gate first. Behind him followed Spike's two keepers.

Moaning slightly, Benjamin began to roll onto his side. Then, as his keeper-bear knelt to get hold of him, Benjamin rolled the other way. As he did so, he deliberately flung up a red-stained arm and brushed it across the keeper-bear's snout.

That snout promptly twitched. The bear's eyes clouded over in suspicion. He rubbed a paw against Benjamin's arm, then licked it.

'Not-this blood-spill!' he growled loudly. 'This root-beet!'

The other two keeper-bears looked at each other. Now they knelt, each studying Spike's red-stained leg. 'And am-this squash-tomato!' exclaimed one. 'Can-me pips-see!'

This was the moment Benjamin had been waiting for. As the keeper-bears all looked up towards the gallery to see what King Antonius and Queen Dearie wanted them to do next, he scrambled to his feet and raced for the open fighting-pit gate.

'Run, Spike!' he screamed.

'I'm right behind you!' yelled Spike.

'Them-stop!' growl-howled King Antonius and Queen Dearie together.

But they were too late. Hardly before the keeper-bears had begun to lumber after them, Benjamin and Spike had reached the open gate. Benjamin dived through. Moments later, Spike dived through – and stopped.

'What are you waiting for?' shouted Benjamin.

His burly keeper-bear, stirred by the fear of what punishment the king and queen might send his way, had started to give chase. Already he was halfway across the pit floor. But still Spike didn't move – until, just as the keeper-bear was close enough, he pushed the heavy fighting-pit gate with all his might. The keeper-bear ran into it with a loud clang, then collapsed in a large heap.

'That's what I was waiting for, matey!' shouted Spike.

Unable to climb over or go round the flattened keeper-bear, the other two were having to try and drag him aside. Spike had bought them extra time to get away.

Casting off their bear's masks and false claws as they went, Benjamin and Spike ran along the dismal passageway which led away from the fighting-pit. Benjamin's mind was racing almost as fast as his legs. Where could they go to now? The passageway they were in led only back to the lonely-den. That would be no use. How had King Antonius come and gone?

Within a few paces that question was answered. Set into the thick wall of the passageway was the foot of a circular staircase. Benjamin skidded to a halt, with Spike beside him. Where did it lead? To the royal chambers, perhaps? That could be dangerous – but did they have much choice?

A sudden clang from the direction of the fighting-pit made Benjamin's mind up for him. The keeper-bears had finally forced open the gate. They were coming.

'This way!' cried Benjamin.

And so, with the growls of the chasing keeper-bears growing ever stronger, he and Spike began racing up the circular staircase to wherever it might lead them.

LYING LOW

Up the staircase they raced, round and round, their feet scraping on the ancient steps, until soon – too soon – they reached the top and burst out into a large, square area that Benjamin immediately recognised. The area was deserted, except for one thing: the figure of a never-move on a pedestal in the middle. Rosetta Willowthin.

The staircase hadn't led them away. It had only led them up – and back. The archway through which Benjamin had passed when he'd first discovered the fighting-pit was just a few paces away. Which meant...

'Spike!' he cried. 'That's the way to the fighting-pit gallery. If they all start coming out...'

Sudden sounds of movement beyond the archway told Benjamin that that was exactly what was about to happen. Delayed firstly by watching the two fighting-saps make their escape, then by their bet-settling, the watching bears would soon be pouring out through the archway.

'Rosetta,' gasped Benjamin. 'Help us! What's the

quickest way out of Bearkingdom-Palace? The two of us have got to get away.'

Rosetta didn't answer, nor did she point. Her eyes flickered, but that was all.

'The *two* of us?' frowned Spike. 'Ain't Squawker here as well? What about her?' 'Squawker' was Spike's nickname for Mops.

'Yes, she's here,' said Benjamin. 'But — oh, Spike, she's changed. She wouldn't even help me when I was starving.'

'Then she'll have had a good reason, matey,' said Spike firmly. 'Squawker waited for you when we got away from the Howling-Tower. You just *can't* run away from here without her.'

'I'm not sure she'll want to come.'

'That'll be up to her. But we've got to ask her, you *know* we have.'

Spike was right. They couldn't run from the palace without finding Mops first. But where was she? In their quarters? In Queen Dearie's chambers, sprawled on her velvet cushion practising her writing? Out in the garden with Cringe and Simper? Benjamin had no idea. But...though he didn't know where Mops was, he definitely *did* know where she was going to be later on.

'Rosetta,' he hissed urgently. 'Do you know where the banquet-chamber is?'

The never-move's eyes flickered again. But this time she also gave the slightest of nods.

'Where? Tell me!'

From beyond the archway the noise was growing louder. King Antonius and Queen Dearie were obviously leading the way, for the queen's voice carried through to them clearly. 'Some-bear catch-me hair-red-that! And bruiser-big-that! Want-me-them head-sliced!'

'Rosetta!' cried Benjamin. 'Please!'

'Left, left, right, right, left,' said the never-move between clenched teeth. 'And be careful,' she whispered as Benjamin and Spike raced away.

Left-left-right-right-left they went, along the Bearkingdom-Palace corridors uuntil they reached the opening into a large, brightly-lit chamber. They shrank back into a nearby alcove.

'That's got to be it,' whispered Benjamin. 'The banquet-chamber'.

'I reckon you're right,' replied Spike, as a flunky-bear waddled past with a tray of golden food bowls.

They crept out and risked peering into the square-shaped chamber. It was huge. Even so, the whole floor had been carpeted with the most expensive flower petals. Every little bit of the walls had been covered with rich layers of ferns and vines and pine cones. As for the bright light, that was being shed by the hundreds of jewel-encrusted torches suspended from the chamber's roof.

'Mops is going to be here later,' said Benjamin.

'Yeah?' Spike took another quick look at the empty banquet-room, still with much lavish preparation to be done. 'Doing what?'

'Showing off. Queen Dearie's taught her to write. If we can find a place to hide we might be able to attract her attention.'

Spike pointed. 'How about under there?'

Round the four walls were mounds of plump cushions for the bears to loll on while they feasted. In front of the cushions were four long rows of low tables. Each table was covered by a white cloth which dangled over the sides and front, hiding the space beneath – a space, as Spike had realised, just about large enough to hide a couple of boys so long as they breathed in a bit.

Benjamin nodded. He waited until the flunky-bear helping prepare the banquet-chamber was busy concentrating on putting his golden food bowls in precisely the right spots on the shimmering white cloths. Then, with Spike close behind, he slid down and out of sight beneath the nearest banqueting table.

Flat on their fronts, Benjamin and Spike began to crawl the length of the table. This took some time. They often had to stop, their hearts in their mouths, as they heard a flunky-bear draw close and lay something on the table just above their heads. Not only that; when the chamber sounded as though it might be flunky-free, Benjamin would pause and ask Spike to tell him about how he'd come to fall into the clutches of Bearon Weimar. The story slowly emerged.

'Bad luck matey, that's what it was. After leaving Squawker waiting for you, I'd got away nicely. Saw a cart carrying a huge pile of straw, didn't I? So when the driver-bear weren't looking I jumped on, burrowed into the pile and pulled the hole closed behind me. Great!'

'What happened then?' asked Benjamin. 'What was the bad luck?'

'Well, the first bit was me falling asleep. We'd been going ages and it was all warm and cosy and...' Spike shrugged. 'Anyway, I woke up to find we'd stopped – and a couple of bears were unloading the straw! So I burrowed a bit further in and hoped they wouldn't do the whole load in one go. That's when I got me second bit of bad luck.'

'What was that?'

'One of the unloaders stuck his claw in me backside. I yelled. They hauled me out and marched me off to what's-his-name...'

'Bearon Weimar,' said Benjamin.

'Whatever,' said Spike. 'He takes a look at me and mutters something about being a bruiser-big. Next thing I know I'm being kitted out with a set of claws and having to fight for something to eat.'

They'd crawled to the very end of the long table they were under. But Benjamin wasn't planning to stop there. Before they ducked out of sight he'd noticed that the table which ran across the top end of the banquet-chamber was slightly different to the other three. It was slightly higher and the cushions behind it were much plumper. Benjamin hoped that meant it was the table to be used by the most important bears such as King Antonius, Queen Dearie, Chancellor Bruno, Bearon Weimar and the other bearons.

Crawling carefully round the corner, Benjamin now led the way beneath this top table. As they moved, he briefly told Spike his story.

'My father is trapped on that galley-royal, Spike. And my mother is a never-move won by Bearon Weimar in a bet...' As he said the words Benjamin was struck by a sudden thought. 'You know where his den is!'

Spike shook his head. 'I wish I did. I slept nearly all the way, matey – remember? I can tell you what it looks like, but not where it is' He gave a deep sigh. 'Same old story. I'm going to be no help.'

'You already have helped, Spike,' said Benjamin. 'If it wasn't for you, I'd have run and left Mops behind.'

He'd stopped crawling. They'd reached what Benjamin thought was close to the very centre of the top table. Here, he reckoned, would be where King Antonius and Queen Dearie would take their places – and wherever the queen was, Mops wouldn't be far away.

'Wait till Squawker sees me,' said Spike. He smiled, as if remembering past times. 'She'll get the shock of her life!'

CHANCELLOR BRUNO'S PLOT

Had Mops been in earshot, she might well have replied to Spike, 'I've already had quite enough shocks for one day, thank you very much!'

Left in the care of Cringe and Simper while King Antonius and Queen Dearie had gone off to watch the sap-fight, she'd done nothing but worry. They'd taken her, along with the rest of the pet-saps, out into the palace gardens. There she'd tried to practise her words, but it had been no good. She'd been able to think of nothing but what might be happening to poor Benjamin.

Then, even worse, the gardens began to fill with bears. Spilling out from the palace, they were all talking angrily about the fight they'd just seen. As the bears roamed around, Mops overheard snatches of conversation that were both chilling and confusing.

'Thought-me over-plenty blood-spill!'

'Sap-cheats.'

'Fight-pretending!'

'Pretend-not Queen Dearie when caught-them!

Want-me to there-be when head-them-sliced!'

What had happened? Had Benjamin won or lost? Had there been blood spilled or not? Had he escaped or not? Was the queen going to have his head cut off or not?

Mops couldn't bear it any longer. She wanted to cry her heart out but only in private. Waiting until Cringe and Simper were busy attending to guest-bears, she ran towards the one place she thought would be quiet: the enclosed garden where Benjamin had led her on the fateful day he punched Queen Dearie on her wet snout.

Mops scurried through the archway in the garden's claw-clipped hedge. Inside, all was quiet, the only sound the scrunching of expensive and perfectly round stones beneath her feet. She ran on, until she reached the grotto containing the empty never-move pedestal where Benjamin had so desperately hoped to find his mother. Once there, she crouched down and prepared to have a really good cry.

What stopped her was the sound of claws on stones. Kneeling up, Mops peered over towards the archway. A bear had just padded furtively through it — a bear with a large chain of office twinkling against fur of silvery-grey, a muzzle of pure white and (though Mops could only hear them) nine jet-black claws. Bearon Weimar.

No sooner had he slipped into the shelter of the tall hedge than another bearon arrived. His name was Bearon Herault. He was huge, one of the biggest bears

Mops had ever seen. He had a curious bald patch in the stubby fur beneath his chin. This he scratched worriedly until he saw Bearon Weimar skulking in the shadow of the hedge. He hurried across to join him. Together, they began to pad silently round the outer paw-path.

Bearon Drachenloch, a thin and shifty-looking bear with twitching ears and ever-fluttering paws, arrived next. He was followed moments later by the arrival of bearon number four, Bearon Sudbury, a bear with a face like a thunderstorm. Sudbury joined Drachenloch and together the pair also set off round the outer paw-path – but in the opposite direction to Weimar and Herault.

How odd, thought Mops. It was almost as if the two separate pairs of bearons had arranged to meet each other in secret. No! she then realised. As if all *four* of the bearons had arranged to meet. For the two pairs had swung away from the outer paw-path and were now showing every sign of heading for the same spot in the garden: the quiet grotto where she now was!

Mops thought fast. What should she do? Run for it? None of them would be likely to stop her. But she wanted to stay and listen. They might have something to say that would give her news of Benjamin – however awful that might be. Hide then? Perhaps she should get out of the grotto and hide behind some of the large bushes growing nearby. But then she wouldn't be able to hear what was being said. No, thought Mops, there was nothing else for it but to find a hiding place in the grotto itself. After all, if the bearons spotted her, they wouldn't think for a moment that she'd understood what they'd said. She'd probably get a very painful cuffing though.

The trouble was, she almost certainly *would* be spotted. The grotto was quiet and secluded – but with four large bears packed inside there wasn't going to be much room for a girl to hide. Correction: *five* large bears. For through the archway entrance had just come the scar-faced figure of none other than Chancellor Bruno. Looking a little flustered, he was loping straight for the grotto.

Behind the never-move pedestal, Mops came to a quick decision. If she couldn't hide outside the grotto, and there was no room inside, then there was the only spot she could think of that would give her a chance of remaining undetected: the never-move pedestal itself. Not behind it – but *on* it! She would take the risk of pretending to be a never-move!

By the time an agitated Chancellor Bruno and the four furtive bearons had converged on the grotto, Mops was in position. She was standing daintily, gazing out into the depths of the garden with her right hand above her eyes as if she was shielding them from the sun. Not a muscle – apart from those in her pounding heart – was moving.

And it worked. So preoccupied were the five bears that, even though Mops wasn't stone-painted, not one of them gave her a second glance. They came straight to the purpose of their secret meeting.

'King Antonius go-must,' growled Chancellor Bruno. 'Still-we agreed-all?'

'Agreed!' murmured the bearons in unison.

Chancellor Bruno looked at Bearon Weimar. 'Bet-that in fighting-pit was straw-last. Thousand-hundred! Where find-him rounds-so-many?'

'Know-you-that,' glowered Bearon Sudbury, his face growing darker as he spoke, 'Up-raised inclaw-tax.'

This made some sort of sense to Mops. Her previous owner had forever been complaining about this inclaw-tax. As she'd discovered by listening to Queen Dearie, each and every bear in the land had to pay it to the bearon who looked after the part of Bear Kingdom in which they lived. It was Chancellor Bruno's job to gather it all together for King Antonius to spend wisely and well. But, as she and Benjamin had seen everywhere they looked, the king, with the help of Queen Dearie, had just frittered it away.

'Money-more!' exclaimed Bearon Drachenloch. His paws fluttered with rage. 'Has had-him money-enough!'

Rubbing the bald spot on his chin, Bearon Herault now brought the meeting back to the point. 'Agreed-we-am. The king go-must. But about-what the queen?'

'Her well-as,' said Chancellor Bruno. 'Agreed-all?'

'Agreed!' nodded the four bearons solemnly.

Chancellor Bruno's scarred face carried a knowing look as he asked next, 'Who-then should King-be?'

'Nominate-me Chancellor Bruno,' said Bearon Drachonloch at once, his voice as smooth as treacle.

Bearon Weimar nodded vigorously. 'Agree-me. All favour-in?'

'Aye!' shouted Bearon Sudbury, just beating Bearon Herault to it.

Chancellor Bruno permitted himself a smile. 'Accept-me wishes-your.'

Up on her pedestal, Mops felt a shiver of fear. It was just what she and Benjamin had heard Chancellor Bruno discussing with the galley-master when they were hiding in the root-rum barrel. The evil, scar-faced bear had been planning this all along.

Ears twitching wildly, the impulsive Bearon Drachenloch now asked, 'When happen-this?'

'Soon-very,' smiled the chancellor. 'During Banquet-Royal.'

The four Bearons gasped in surprise. 'How-do?' asked Bearon Sudbury, his wide eyes in his thunderous face looking like two moons in the night sky.

Chancellor Bruno laid a single claw against his black snout. 'Secret-my,' he murmured. He drew himself upright. 'But must-me ready-get.' With that he left the grotto, loping quickly across the enclosed garden and out through the archway.

Left alone, the four bearons had little to say to each other. Mops had a good idea why. If Chancellor Bruno's plot succeeded, then he would be in their debt. As the new king, he would have the power to choose one of them to take his place as Chancellor. And, of course, he would want to make sure the bearons all kept quiet about what had happened. By giving them presents, perhaps...

As Mops was about to find out, this second thought was certainly going through the mind of the white-muzzled Bearon Weimar. The other three bearons had drifted away one by one. Instead of following them, though, he began to pad quietly around the grotto.

'Keep-me my hair-red never-move certain-for,' Mops heard him murmur from a little distance away.

'Maybe even another-me-get,' she heard from a little closer.

'A pretty-pink, perhaps,' she heard from very near. 'Nicer-much than stone-painteds.'

And then that white muzzle was right in front of her as she heard him say, 'Like...one-this.'

Me! realised Mops to her horror. He is talking about me!

Standing daintily with her hand shielding her eyes while the four bearons and Chancellor Bruno plotted had been hard enough. But now it became almost impossible.

First, Mops's eyes dipped...to see Bearon Weimar's own black eyes glittering at the thought of adding another never-move to his collection. Then her arms began to tremble as the silvery-grey bear leaned forward and she wanted so much to push him away. But that was as nothing to the reaction of her right leg when Bearon Weimar stretched out his four-clawed paw to stroke it. For at that moment, Mops's resolve cracked completely.

'Don't you dare!' she screeched, lashing out with her foot to kick the paw away.

The astonished bear howled in pain. (Mops, by pure luck, had landed her kick on the tender spot where his missing claw used to be.) He staggered backwards, trying to work out exactly what had happened. Never before had a never-move moved in his presence – and certainly never kicked him.

Mops seized her chance. Leaping from the pedestal as if it were a hot plate she hit the ground running. Before Bearon Weimar could stop her she was racing back to where Cringe and Simper had left her. She was greeted with open paws. The worried flunky-bears had been looking for her.

'On-come!' cried Cringe.

Simper was already on the move. 'Queen Dearie off-you-show!' called the flunky-bear over his shoulder.

And with that, they led Mops back into Bearkingdom-Palace to get her ready for the Banquet-Royal.

THE DEADLY BANQUET

Benjamin and Spike were finding their hiding spot increasingly uncomfortable. There wasn't much room to spare beneath the top table in the banquet-chamber. Benjamin could only get himself up onto his knees if he bent himself almost double. Spike couldn't even manage that. All he could do was stretch out his larger body near enough flat on the ground.

And so it was Spike, not Benjamin, who'd peered through the tiny gap between two sections of table cloth and seen the comings and goings of the various flunky-bears as they brought in piece after piece of glittering tableware. It was Spike also who'd reported, after what felt like an age, that the preparation of the chamber seemed to have finished.

'How do you know?' whispered Benjamin.

'The flunkies have all gone,' replied Spike, only to correct himself at once as he saw a lone flunky return. 'Tell a lie. There's one.' No sooner had he said that, than he had to correct himself again. 'Make that two. A new one's turned up. Nasty looking one, an' all. Got a big scar on his head.'

On hearing this, Benjamin twisted himself round so that he too could see through the gap in the tablecloth. He recognised the scar-faced bear at once.

'It's Chancellor Bruno!' he whispered.

'The one you reckon wants to be king?' asked Spike. During their wait beneath the table, Benjamin had told him about what he and Mops had overheard the Chancellor saying to the galley-master.

Benjamin held a finger to his lips. Chancellor Bruno was padding closer to them, the flunky-bear beside him. By the time they stopped, the pair were so close to the table that Benjamin could have reached out a hand and touched them.

'All ready-is?' he heard Chancellor Bruno say.

The reply he got was high-pitched and sounded very nervous. 'Sure-you this-about, sir? Can-nothing wrong-go?'

It was a voice that Benjamin was sure he'd heard before. Where? Who was it? Parting the tablecloth slightly he peered out and up. It was Briny, the galley-bear! But...dressed as a flunky? He could think of only one explanation. King Antonius and Queen Dearie must have told the galley-master to send some of his crew along to the palace to help with all the work for the Banquet-Royal. *That* was why the galley-master knew of Chancellor Bruno's plan – because his galley-bears would be on the spot to help him to carry it out! Benjamin quickly ducked back out of sight as Chancellor Bruno answered Briny's question with a growl-sneer.

'Can-nothing wrong-go. Obtained-us poison-finest.'

'P-poison?' stammered Briny.

'Here-take.' From beneath the table, Benjamin and Spike heard the faintest scratch of claw on glass as the Chancellor passed a small bottle to the trembling Briny. 'Empty-you-some King Antonius's goblet-fourth of juice-grape.'

'Goblet-fourth?' echoed Briny. 'Not goblet-first? It-get done-and-over with.'

'The king must suspect-not.' Chancellor Bruno chuckled crudely. 'By goblet-fourth will-he know-not what is on-going.'

'What-if stops-he at goblet-third?' asked Briny.

'The king stops-*never* at goblet-third,' growled Chancellor Bruno. 'Nor the queen.'

'The queen? Queen Dearie poison-gets too?'

'Course-of,' answered the chancellor. 'Married-they-are. Promise-them to everything-share!' He suddenly stepped away from the table. 'Go-now. And forget-not. Goblet-fourth!'

Things now began to happen.

A stream of flunky-bears (heard, if not seen, by Benjamin and Spike) swept two-by-two into the chamber and took up positions around the square of tables. Another flunky-bear came in then, alone. This one was carrying a long, curved blow-horn. Raising it to his mouth, the flunky took a deep breath and blew hard. Dah da-da-da-da-da dah!

'The Banquet-Royal served-is!' boomed a deep-voiced flunky-bear near the entrance.

There was a short delay. Then guests began to enter, also two-by-two. Each time, the deep-voiced flunky-bear called out the guests' names.

'Honour-His, the Chancellor Bruno!'

'Bearon and Lady-bear Weimar!'

'Bearon and Lady-bear Drachenloch!'

And so it went on, until finally the blow-horn sounded again and the shout-flunky shouted into its echoes, 'Their Majesties-Royal, King Antonius and Queen Dearie!'

As the king and queen marched regally into the banquet-chamber, the blow-horn sounded yet again. This time its fanfare was joined by the thump-thump of the guest-bears drumming their rear paws in time with King Antonius's and Queen Dearies's progress towards the places of honour at the very centre of the top table.

Finally, the blow-trumpet ceased blowing. The paw-thumping stopped. And the unmistakeable voice of King Antonius commanded, 'Seated-be!'

Beneath the top table, Benjamin and Spike heard the squeaks of plump bear-bottoms landing heavily on cushions. A rear paw with a gold bracelet round its ankle was thrust suddenly under the hem of the tablecloth, making Benjamin move sharply to avoid it. Beside him, Spike looked fearful.

'I hope Squawker turns up soon, matey,' he whispered. 'I don't feel safe under here.'

'I hope so too, Spike,' replied Benjamin. He thought, but didn't say: and I hope it'll be worth it when she does.

A series of sounds from above their heads drove the thought from his mind. First came a succession of clunks, as if huge bowls of the finest food had been deposited in front of the guests. When the bears began to eat, Benjamin heard the unmistakeable sounds of chomping jaws and smacking lips. Finally came the sounds of liquid being poured – then a loud slurping.

King Antonius had begun to drink his first goblet of juice-grape.

Mops was a bundle of nerves. How she'd managed to walk into the banquet-chamber alongside Queen Dearie without her legs giving way beneath her she really didn't know.

The procession had been very grand, but had passed in a blur – mainly because of what she'd overheard. King Antonius and Queen Dearie may have been waving grandly to the assembled guests, but they'd been talking to each other as they moved.

'Catch-you-yet those fighting-saps yet?' Queen Dearie had asked sharply.

'No,' King Antonius had replied irritably. 'Disappeared-them into air-thin.'

This news had filled Mops with delight. Benjamin had got away! But...the queen had said 'fighting-*saps*' not 'fighting-*sap*'. Benjamin hadn't only got away, he'd found somebody to escape with. In that moment Mops had never felt more alone.

'Want-me caught-them!' the queen had insisted as she'd reached the top table and shoved Mops ahead of her.

'Worry-not, petal-my,' King Antonius had answered. 'Catch-me-them if thing-last do-me.'

Never have you spoken a truer word, thought Mops as she flopped down onto one of the cushions laid out behind the top table. If the plotters she'd overheard were successful then this banquet-royal might well be the last thing that King Antonius did. Her nerves – already jangling at the thought of her writing demonstration – weren't improved by knowing that something was going to happen. What would the plotters do? How would they do it?

These thoughts were uppermost in her mind as the banquet began. She didn't even enjoy the odd treat that Queen Dearie tossed her way. She and King Antonius were looking slightly more cheerful, though. They'd clinked goblets and said 'up-bottoms' to each other more than once.

Soon the king was snapping his claws and calling

over a flunky-bear whose face looked vaguely familiar to Mops. 'My goblet-empty,' he ordered. 'The queen's goblet-empty. Up-fill, quick-double!'

'Yes, Majesty-your,' said Briny filling both their goblets to the brim again.

It was then – as King Antonius took a large gulp from his second goblet of juice-grape – that Mops felt something begin to crawl over her ankle.

'That's number two,' Benjamin had hissed when he'd heard King Antonius asking for his goblet to be refilled.

But Spike hadn't been listening to him. His attention had been elsewhere. Flat on his front, Spike's eyes had been fixed on a point just beyond the crouching Benjamin's left shoulder. It was as Benjamin had heard the grape-juice being poured into the king's goblet that Spike had pointed – and uttered a single, whispered, word, 'Squawker!'

Benjamin twisted his head round – and then saw what Spike had seen: a pair of pink-clad ankles, poking under the tablecloth alongside Queen Dearie's clawed feet. Twisting himself round completely, he edged along beneath the table until he was within touching distance of Mops's leg. He had to let her know they were there. That way, when Chancellor Bruno's nasty plan began to unfold, she'd be able to run with them in the chaos that followed. If she wanted to, that was.

And so, with the tip of his finger, he began the

tickling that made Mops think something was crawling over her ankle.

To Benjamin's dismay, Mops did no more than twitch and wriggle her foot. She didn't lift the tablecloth to see what the cause of the itch was. He tickled her ankle again. This time Mops not only twitched and wriggled her foot, she also switched the other foot across to give it a scratch. But still she didn't look under the tablecloth.

'Have one more go,' urged Spike.

Benjamin didn't get the chance. For as he reached his hand out towards Mops's ankle, it rose upwards, disappearing from the floor as if she'd been lifted bodily upwards by an invisible hand. She had – but by a paw, not a hand: Benjamin and Spike heard a solid clonk above their heads as Mops was dropped feet-first onto the top table so that every bear in the banquet-chamber could see her. They then heard two growl-shouts, 'Bearons, she-bears and gentle-bears.' growl-shouted Queen Dearie. Have-me you-for entertainment-wondrous!' 'A writing-sap!'

And King Antonius growl-shouted for his third goblet of juice-grape.

Standing on the rough wooden surface of the top table, Mops couldn't help feeling a little pleased to hear the bubble of impressed ooh-growls that followed Queen Dearie's announcement. After all, she told herself, if

170

Benjamin Wildfire *has* escaped then what have I got left? A life in Bearkingdom-Palace with King Antonius and Queen Dearie — or with Chancellor Bruno. Either way, if that was going to be the case, then the more popular she was the better.

Queen Dearie had already beckoned two flunky-bears into the centre of the chamber. One held a pot of ink-blue, the other a scratch-pad large enough for the whole audience to see. Moments later a third flunky-bear was lifting Mops from the table and standing her in front of the pad.

'Sap-this,' Queen Dearie repeated, just in case any of her guests had missed it the first time, 'write-can!'

The ooh-growls faded into a disbelieving silence as this claim sank in. A sap who could write? It was unheard of. A good number of the cubs currently leaving the Bear Kingdom's learning-caverns couldn't do that!

Waiting for her first command, Mops's nerves returned. She was going to fail, she knew she was. Her hand was shaking so much she'd make blots everywhere. It was no comfort to see that Queen Dearie was feeling nervous as well. She was waiting until a flunky-bear had filled her and King Antonius's goblets for the third time. Only when this had been done, and she'd taken a big sip, did the queen finally say, very slowly, 'Pinkie-pops...write-you "good"!'

Mops dipped her shaking nail into the ink-blue.

Tensing herself for the scratchy sound which always made her shiver, Mops pressed her nail against the pad. Slowly, carefully – and to her great relief without making a single blot – she wrote the letters G-O-O-D. As the scratch-pad was paraded round the chamber, the bears gawped at Mops's writing in astonishment.

Queen Dearie beamed. Even King Antonius put down his drinking goblet for a moment to clap his paws loudly. 'Full-wonder, Pinkie-pops!' cried the queen, more for the audience's benefit than anything else. She switched back to the painfully slow way of speaking that she thought Mops needed. 'Pinkie-pops… write-you "bad"!'

To a wild burst of applause, Mops did just as she was asked.

The queen took another sip from her goblet. Beside her, the king did more than that. He took a long gulp and still had his goblet up to his lips when Queen Dearie slowly told Mops, 'Write-you…"queen"!'

Mops bit her lip, concentrated hard – and wrote 'Q-U-E-E-N'. The applause had hardly died down before she was getting another burst for writing 'K-I-N-G'.

'Full-wonder again, Pinkie-pops!' trilled Queen Dearie. She turned proudly to her astonished audience. 'Comes-now the light-high! Sap-pet-this remember-can words-*two*!' She swung back to Mops, and said carefully, 'Write-you "food" and "drink!"'

All eyes were now on Mops as she dipped her writing

nail into the pot of ink-blue and turned to the scratch-pad. Not a morsel of food was eaten as she carefully wrote the letters 'F-O-O-D'. And, as she followed this by writing the letters 'D-R-I-N-K', so engrossed were the watching bears that not one of them drank a drop – not even King Antonius. In his case, though, it wasn't just because he was spellbound at Mops's ability. The king's goblet was empty. And so, when Mops had finished and was being applauded from all sides, King Antonius wasted no time in putting that particular matter right.

'Calls-this for celebration-drink!' he roared. 'Need-me goblet-fill!'

A delighted Queen Dearie promptly drained her own goblet. 'Also-me!' she cried.

'The fourth goblet, Spike!' hissed Benjamin.

On hearing the shouts of King Antonius and Queen Dearie, he'd felt an odd thrill. The thought of them being poisoned was horrible, of course, but if that was the sort of thing that went on amongst the rulers of Bear Kingdom then there wasn't much he could do about it. Sap-fighting was pretty horrible too. What had thrilled him was the thought that any minute now there'd be complete pandemonium in the banquet-chamber. In the chaos he and Spike would be able to leap out of hiding, grab Mops and run for it.

He thought of twisting his cramped body round to

173

peer out through the gap at the front of the tablecloth, but decided against it. There was no point in taking risks at this stage.

And so he didn't see Briny the galley-bear, flunky-bear, whatever he was, glance nervously in the direction of Chancellor Bruno.

He didn't see the scar-faced bear give the slightest of nods.

He didn't see Briny weave his way through to the top table.

Neither did Benjamin see Briny fill the goblets of King Antonius and Queen Dearie with juice-grape containing enough poison to kill a bear with just one sip.

And he definitely didn't see the delighted queen push a third, much smaller, goblet forward just as Mops was returning to her place in triumph.

No.

All Benjamin heard was the queen saying to Mops, 'Deserve-you treat-special!' Then to Briny, 'Pour-you a juice-grape for Pinkie-pops!'

Mops watched her drink being poured. Her nerves gone, the applause of the assembled bears still ringing in her ears, she was ready for anything.

And she'd never tried juice-grape before...

Beneath the table, all thought of staying hidden was

forgotten. Benjamin knew that if he didn't do something quickly it would be too late. Balling his fists, he hammered furiously on the underside of the table.

'Don't drink it, Mops!' he screamed.

Beside him, Spike did some hammering too. Reaching forward, he thumped his fist hard down on the manicured rear paw that Queen Dearie was still dangling beneath the tablecloth. At the same time he yelled, 'It's poisoned, Squawker!'

The shock of hearing that nickname again stopped Mops before she'd even taken a single sip from her goblet. The surprise – and pain – of having her paw thumped stopped Queen Dearie. And the sight of Benjamin and Spike crambling out from beneath the table stopped the king. Pointing his poisoned goblet at them, Antonius didn't sip – he roared.

'The fighting-saps! Them-seize!'

Briny the galley-bear, slowly realising that if King Antonius and Queen Dearie dropped dead because of a poisoned drink then it could well be the drink-server who got blamed, acted at once. Delighted at the chance of showing that he was really a devoted servant of the king and queen, he made a grab for Benjamin.

Benjamin ducked out of his reach, at the same time yelling at Mops, 'It's a plot! Chancellor Bruno has poisoned those drinks!'

Briny now made a grab for Spike – only to get a painful shoulder in the stomach as Spike barged into him, shouting, 'Chuck it away, Squawker!'

'Them-catch!' roared King Antonius again.

Briny, badly winded, dived for Benjamin again. This time he was more successful. Even as Benjamin tried to snatch the small goblet away from Mops, he found Briny's large furry arms wrapping round him and holding him fast. He struggled and kicked, but it was useless. Other flunky-bears had hurried forward to help out. Within moments he was being held tight by a dozen paws. So too was Spike. Their escape bid was over.

'Mops!' cried Benjamin, desperately. 'Help us!'

Stunned, Mops looked at Benjamin. She looked at Spike. She looked down at the three goblets of juice-grape. Poisoned? Could that be right? There *was* a plot, she'd heard Chancellor Bruno and the bearons discussing it. But what she hadn't heard was how the king was to be removed. Chancellor Bruno had said only, 'Secret-my.' Was *poison* his secret?

The scar-faced bear answered that question himself. Seated a few places further along the top table, he now called out, 'Up-drink, Majesty-your!'

King Antonius hadn't touched his goblet while Benjamin and Spike were being captured. Now he reached out and took it between his paws. It was still full. In spite of all Benjamin's hammering on the bottom of the table, not a drop of the poisoned drink had been spilled from the sturdy goblet.

'Idea-good, Chancellor!' said the king. 'Then have-we-some fighting-sap head-slicing!'

Queen Dearie growl-laughed delightedly. 'Drink-me to idea-that!'

As they raised their goblets towards their lips, Mops did the only thing she could think of to stop them.

'Wahhh!' she screeched at the top of her voice. 'Wah! Wah! Wahhh!'

It worked. Both the king and queen put their goblets down in surprise. Now what? thought Mops. For the first time in her life she found herself thinking how useful it would be if bears could understand human speech. She'd be able to explain everything. But they couldn't, so...so...she would use writing instead!

Mops raced across to where her scratch-pad was leaning against the wall. Dragging it across to the top table, she let it fall flat on the floor. There, one by one, she pointed at three of the words she'd written during her demonstration: KING...DRINK...BAD

Then, just in case the king hadn't got the message, she repeated the exercise with a different first word: QUEEN...DRINK...BAD

King Antonius frowned. His dark eyes clouded over. He lifted his goblet, tilted his snout – and sniffed.

'Has drink-this smell-funny,' he growled. He took Queen Dearie's goblet and sniffed at that. 'Here-same!'

A deathly silence fell across the banquet-chamber.

The bearons looked nervously at each other. Briny looked nervously at Chancellor Bruno. And that scar-faced bear looked *very* nervously at the king – because, goblet in paw, King Antonius was moving menacingly his way.

'Tell-you-me "up-drink", Chancellor,' said the king suspiciously. 'Well, have-me manners-good. So... you-after.' And with that he held the poisoned goblet out for Chancellor Bruno to take.

Chancellor Bruno did so, held it for a moment... then said coolly, 'Have-me idea-better. It-give the fighting-saps.'

This piece of clever thinking was immediately helped along by the stupid and unsuspecting Queen Dearie. 'Idea-splendid!' she cried. 'If die-them know-we poisoned-is. If die-them-not then have-we-them head-sliced!'

Chancellor Bruno handed the poisoned goblet to Briny, who had just about recovered from the thump in the stomach that Spike had given him. He took it. Slowly he padded towards Benjamin and Spike, still being held firm in the middle of the banquet-chamber floor by flunky-bears. The two friends twisted and turned but couldn't break free. Briny was within touching distance...

'Don't you dare poison them!' screamed Mops.

Heaving the heavy scratch-pad up onto its side, she whirled it across the floor at Briny's legs.

The galley/flunky-bear saw it coming. Leaping into the air he let it slide harmlessly beneath his feet. But the stupid bear had momentarily forgotten that he was holding a goblet – and a brimming goblet at that. As he landed again, the juice-grape sloshed all over his fur.

In a total panic (and forgetting that poison only works if you swallow it) Briny reeled backwards, bellowing with fear. 'Have-me poisoned-been!'

'What?' growled King Antonius. This was all the proof he needed. Pointing at Chancellor Bruno he bawled, 'Him-arrest!'

'No, *them*-arrest!' roared Chancellor Bruno, pointing back at the king and queen. 'Guilty-them of robbery-daylight!'

'Yes, them-arrest!' echoed Bearons Drachenloch, Herault and Sudbury with pointing claws.

It was Bearon Weimar who came out with something different. 'Her-grab!' he bawled, pointing his four-clawed paw at Mops. 'Want-me-her as never-move! Reward-me-offer!'

The whole banquet-chamber erupted into a blur of fighting bears.

The flunky-bears who worked in Bearkingdom-Palace and were loyal to King Antonius and Queen Dearie rushed across to grab Chancellor Bruno.

The other flunkies who, like Briny, worked on the Galley-Royal, rushed in a different direction. Ordered by the galley-master to support the chancellor and the four bearons, most of them now charged towards the king and queen.

Clambering onto the top table to get away from Bearon Weimar, Mops saw that the only flunkies who hadn't moved were those holding Benjamin and Spike. She quickly realised why. It was because in all the instructions roared out, nobody had mentioned fighting-saps. But...they had mentioned her!

Plucking a golden food bowl from the table, Mops took aim at one of the flunkies holding on to Benjamin and let fly. The bowl sailed through the air, to land with a crack just above the flunky's left ear. He howled, looked up – and saw Mops. He nudged his neighbour, and pointed. Mops could almost hear them saying to each other, 'Is-there the writing-sap! Bearon Weimar her-wants! Reward-him-offering!'

Mops was sure that all they needed was a little more persuasion to leave Benjamin and Spike and come for her. So she gave it to them. With an airy wave, she dived off the top table and out of sight on to the mound of cushions behind. Seeing their possible reward vanish had exactly the effect on the flunkies Mops had expected. Releasing Benjamin and Spike, they began pushing and shoving their way through the throng of battling bears and towards her.

'Run for it, Spike!' yelled Benjamin the moment he was released.

'I'm right behind you *again*, matey!' shouted Spike.

Now they, too, began ploughing their way through the fighting bears — but in the opposite direction to the flunkies heading for Mops. They were aiming for the banquet-chamber's exit. With every bear in the place either fighting for the king and queen or fighting for Chancellor Bruno and the bearons, or chasing after Mops, they were totally ignored. In next to no time they'd reached the exit.

Ahead the corridor was clear. There was nothing to stop them getting clean away. Except for one thing. Benjamin skidded to a halt, hope in his heart.

'What are you waiting for?' shouted Spike. 'Let's go!'

'I'm waiting for Mops,' answered Benjamin. 'Just as she waited for me.'

Spike pointed back into the fury of the banquet-chamber. 'But she's right at the back of that lot, an' all them flunkies are after her. How's she going to get out of there?'

'Precisely the same way you got in, I presume,' said an indignant voice. 'By crawling round beneath the tables.'

'Mops!' cried an overjoyed Benjamin as the pink-clad figure emerged from beneath the very table that he and Spike had ducked under when they'd first found the banquet-chamber.

Spike grinned. 'Squawker, you're brainier than you look!'

'I will take that as a compliment,' smiled Mops. 'Now, are we leaving this place or not?'

'Yes, Mops!' cried Benjamin. 'Yes, yes, yes!'

THE GALLEY-MASTER'S KEYS

Benjamin, Mops and Spike raced through the petal-strewn corridors. As they ran, Benjamin wondered how they were going to get past the bear-guards patrolling outside the gold-tipped railings. But, when they burst out into the palace courtyard, there were none to be seen.

'Where have all the guards gone?' shouted Benjamin.

'Inside,' replied Mops as they charged across the courtyard. 'Queen Dearie's orders. She said there was no point them being out here when any bear worth guarding was going to be in the banqueting-chamber. So they're now probably fighting along with everybody else.'

'More importantly,' yelled Spike as they raced out through the wide open gates, 'where are *we* going?'

Benjamin pointed ahead, just beyond the short distance he and Mops had travelled in the gold cart not so many sun-comes before. At the far end of the track they'd been carried down in the golden cart, still berthed at the quay-side, was the Galley-Royal.

'That's where we're going, Spike!' cried Benjamin.

Spike skidded to a halt, his head shaking furiously. 'Oh no, we're not. Not me, matey.'

'But we must. My father's there!'

'I know. But so's that galley-master you told me about. And them galley-bears. They're not gonna catch me and turn me into a galley-sap.'

'Still as gloomy as ever, I see?' sighed Mops. 'They won't catch you, Spike, because they won't be there to catch you. All the galley-bears are in the palace.'

'You're...sure?' said Benjamin.

'About as sure as I can be. Didn't you see how many of those flunkies were wearing those gorgeous little ear-blings? If that isn't a give-away I don't know what is.'

'So...them galley-bears...won't be on that galley-float?' said Spike slowly.

'No!' shouted Mops. 'Spelt "N" and "O"!'

'Then what are we waiting for!' yelled Spike.

Even so, after racing the length of the cart-track and across the open space of the quayside they still stopped cautiously at the foot of the ramp leading up to the Galley-Royal. There, they scoured the upper deck for signs of life. There were none.

Hope rising in his heart, Benjamin led the way up the ramp. There, they checked left and right. All was clear. If it hadn't been for an intermittent rumbling noise coming from somewhere in the depths, they could have been forgiven for thinking that the Galley-Royal had been completely abandoned.

'I want to see my father,' whispered Benjamin.

'Course you do,' murmured Spike. 'You get going. Squawker and me will stay here and keep watch.'

Benjamin wasn't sure it was a good idea for them to separate but so strong was his need to see his father again that he agreed. Leaving Spike and Mops, he hurried to the stairway leading down to the galley-sap deck.

Duncan Wildfire was still there, still chained to both the bench he was on and to Roger Broadback beside him. They were both asleep. At the rear of the deck the awful drum that controlled their rowing speed was silent. Not a single galley-bear was in sight. Scurrying across to his father's side, Benjamin shook him gently awake.

'Father!' he hissed.

Duncan Wildfire's eyes opened blearily, then lit up with joy. 'Benjamin! I've been so worried about you. Where have you been?'

'I'll tell you later, Father,' said Benjamin urgently. Again he checked that they weren't about to be seen. 'Where are all the galley-bears?'

'Ashore,' said Duncan Wildfire. 'They all left just after middle-sun. The galley-master was yelling at them to obey Chancellor Bruno's orders without question.'

That confirmed it. Mops had been right, the galley-bears *had* all been at the palace. And must still be there, fighting on behalf of Chancellor Bruno. In which case...*who* was guarding the Galley-Royal?

'What about the galley-master?' asked Benjamin urgently. 'Did he go too?'

'Nope,' said Roger Broadback, joining the conversation. 'He came down here, made sure we were all securely chained, as if we could be anything else, then staggered off.'

'Complaining about his guts-grumble,' smiled Duncan Wildfire. 'Again.'

Roger Broadback nodded. 'He's been doing a lot of that lately. Ever since you went away, in fact,' he said to Benjamin.

Benjamin laughed. If the galley-master was still complaining about attacks of guts-grumble then there could be only one explanation – the proud grey bear was still taking drinks of root-rum from the barrel that he and Mops had used to wash off their poison-rat! Mixed with the root-rum the poison wasn't strong enough to finish the galley-master off, just make him feel very ill and in serious need of a comfortable lie down. A *comfortable* lie down?

'The keys!' cried Benjamin.

Racing back up to where Spike and Mops were still keeping watch, Benjamin told them what he'd heard from his father and Roger Broadback.

'You got an idea then, matey?' asked Spike.

'Yes, I have!' said Benjamin. 'Follow me!'

The intermittent rumbling noise they'd heard when they'd boarded the Galley-Royal hadn't been coming from just anywhere – it had been coming from the galley-master's alcove. The noise was a mixture of snoring, heavy breathing and growl-groaning.

Peering round the curtain drawn across the alcove's opening, Benjamin could see the galley-master clearly. He no longer looked proud and perfectly-groomed. He looked miserable. His fur was dishevelled. Smelly and nasty-looking stains covered his front, as if he'd been sick…lots of times.

He wasn't lying on his straw bed. He was half-sitting, half-slouching, his back propped up against the wooden wall. But the hook on which Benjamin had hoped to see his keys was empty.

'Oh, no!' whispered Benjamin. 'I was hoping he'd hung his keys up.'

But galley-master's chain was still slung over his shoulder and across his stomach, as if he'd felt so awful he hadn't been able to raise the energy to take it off.

'No problem, matey,' whispered Spike. 'You and Squawker can hold him down while I get them off him.'

'Are you mad?' hissed Mops. 'Even you couldn't lift those keys on your own.'

'They can't be *that* heavy!'

'No? Then look at the size of that hook!'

Spike admitted defeat. 'All right, so it's only the galley-master who's strong enough to lift 'em off,' he said glumly. 'Sorry I spoke.'

But Benjamin wasn't. 'Spike, you're right! We need to

get the galley-master to take those keys off himself!'

Mops arched an eyebrow. 'And how do you propose to do that?'

In just a few words, Benjamin explained. And in even fewer words, Mops and Spike agreed.

'I will do my best,' said Mops, heading one way.

'Me too, matey,' said Spike, heading the other.

Left alone, Benjamin eased himself into the galley-master's alcove. He had to be careful. If the big bear awoke now, there'd be no escape. Benjamin took a couple more steps forward, up to the root-rum barrel. It was almost empty! In drinking more and more in the hope that it would make him feel better, the galley-master had been making himself feel worse and worse.

With increased hope, Benjamin crept forward another couple of paces. He didn't want to hurry – but neither did he have much time. Tiptoeing the final steps forward, he reached the galley-master's side. Being this close made Benjamin feel both frightened and sick. The slumbering bear's lips were parted. His sharp teeth were poking out and a trickle of dribble was running down his cheek. His breath smelled foul.

Slowly, oh-so-slowly, Benjamin now slid the fingers of both hands beneath the key-chain which looped its way over the galley-master's shoulder. The chain was so heavy it felt like it was crushing his fingers. Mops had been right, even Spike would never have been able to lift it. As for himself, it would be completely impossible. But Benjamin's idea didn't call for him to *lift* the chain...only to *slide* it!

Gritting his teeth, Benjamin heaved – and the chain moved! His hopes rising, Benjamin gave it another tug in the direction he wanted. And again. It was nearly there...

Suddenly, the galley-master gave a snort and a jerk. Benjamin caught his breath. If the galley-master turned over now, all would be lost. The bear gave a loud grunt, another jerk...then slumped back in the place where he'd started, his shoulder against the giant hook. With one final heave, Benjamin managed to do what he'd been aiming for all along: slide the weighty chain off the galley-master's shoulder and on to its hook.

All he had to do now was wake the galley-master up. Benjamin was just wondering how he could manage that when he discovered, to his horror, that it wasn't necessary. The galley-master was *already* awake.

For while he'd been snorting and jerking, the foul-smelling bear had also been flicking one bleary eye open. The other bleary eye had followed. And, though his aching body hadn't felt the chain slide off, those two blood-shot eyes had certainly told him that he wasn't as alone as he should be. With an irritated lunge, the galley-master's big right paw looped round to hold Benjamin tight.

'You-got!' he snarled. Slowly, his eyes began to

189

focus. A look of recognition crossed his face. 'The hair-red! Again! Right, drown-me-you time-this and mistake-none!'

The galley-master lurched to his feet, ready to carry out his threat. What stopped him was the sound of a drum beginning to beat. Thump-thump-thump.

That shocked him. But not half as much as hearing the sound change to thump-splash, thump-splash... and feeling the Galley-Royal give a sideways lurch.

The galley-master's mouth fell open. 'Galley-this moving-is,' he muttered to himself. 'But order-me-not speed-full-ahead. Order-me thing-no!'

Confused, bleary-eyed and irritated, the smelly bear hurled Benjamin aside. He would deal with the hair-red later. Unauthorised galley-moving came first on his list.

With an angry shout, he took a step forward – but got no further. For, just as Benjamin had planned, the key chain round his shoulders had tightened on the huge hook to hold him back. Grunting, the galley-master tried to turn and release it. But that only caused the heavy chain to twist round his neck so that he could hardly breathe.

And still the drum was drumming and the Galley-Royal was lurching.

Howling with frustration, the galley-master did the only thing he could to free himself quickly and find out what was going on. He heaved the bulky key-chain over his head. Then, without stopping to lift it from its hook and put it back on again, the galley-master charged outside and headed for the stairway leading to the galley-sap's deck.

It had worked! Benjamin couldn't lift the weighty chain from its hook, of course, but he'd known that. It didn't matter. He only wanted one key, and any key would do. He slid one quickly from the chain. Then he too raced out – but in a different direction to the galley-master. The drumming had stopped. The next part of his plan was about to unfold.

For, as Benjamin well knew, it had been Mops who'd been beating the drum. She'd galloped to the galley-saps' deck straight after leaving Benjamin. There she'd told Duncan Wildfire and the others what was happening. They hadn't needed telling twice. The moment Mops began thumping on the drum, they began heaving on their rowing-poles, splashing them hard down into the dirty, smelly waters of the Winding-River. It was this that had caused the lurching of the Galley-Royal which had shocked the galley-master so much.

Mops now heard the furious bear coming. That wasn't difficult, because he was roaring 'drum-stop!' with every rumbling step. Still Mops carried on pounding her steady beat – up until the moment the galley-master emerged from the stairway at the far end of the deck and she knew he'd seen her. Only then did she act. Throwing aside her drumstick, Mops raced away and up the stairway leading to the main deck.

Benjamin was waiting for her, at the head of the ramp. Within moments they'd been joined by Spike, running up the ramp from the side-quay below.

'All done, matey!'

Spike pointed down at the stout ropes that had been stopping the galley-royal from drifting. It had been quite an effort, but he had managed to complete his part of Benjamin's plan by releasing them from the posts they'd been tied to. Those ropes were now slack instead of taut, their ends dangling in the water.

So where did Benjamin, Mops and Spike race off to next? Nowhere. They simply stood and waited the very short time it took for the galley-master, chasing after Mops, to arrive at the top deck and see them. Even then they didn't move. Well, not very much. Benjamin simply raised his hand, no more than that. But he made sure he raised it high enough for the galley-master to see that Benjamin was holding one of his precious keys.

The furious bear skidded to a halt. This was too much. Never, in all his moons, had one of his keys so much fallen in to the claws of another bear. And yet here one was, in the ugly fingers of a *sap*! All other thoughts – the drumming, the unauthorised movement of the Galley-Royal, even the terrible ache caused by repeated attacks of grumble-guts – were now swept from his mind. Just one overwhelming thought replaced them all. He was going to get that key back.

With a bellow of, 'That me-give!' he charged straight for Benjamin. But still the three friends didn't move. Closer and closer the galley-master lumbered, the wooden deck vibrating beneath his paws, until he was virtually upon them.

Then they moved.

Spike dived to his left. With a terrified squeak, Mops dived to her right. As for the brave Benjamin, he did the thing the galley-master was least expecting, and dived between his pounding paws.

Only then did the bear realise that the three saps had been standing at the head of the ramp. Unable to stop, he careered on, making the ramp shudder as he landed on it. But only for a moment. For down below, the galley-saps were still rowing hard. The galley-royal, its ropes untied by Spike, was moving away from the side-quay. And the end of the ramp had been moving with it.

Having the galley-master land heavily on its top now gave the ramp the final shake it needed to set it free. With a great splash, its bottom end crashed into the water. At the same time, its top end began to fall. Desperately, the galley-master tried to turn back. But, even as he made a despairing dive for the side of the Galley-Royal, the rowing galley-saps made it lurch just that little bit further away. Howling with rage, the galley-master plummeted down into the water with a mighty 'splosh'.

'Bear overboard!' shouted Benjamin joyously.

'You think we should throw him a belt-life?' hooted Spike.

'I think he'll be able to swim to the side, Spike,' said Mops. Then, cupping her hands, she screeched in a very un-Mops-like fashion at the struggling galley-master, 'Good job you haven't still got that dirty great key-chain round your neck, isn't it!'

They watched for a few moments longer, laughing as the galley-master bobbed to the surface with unspeakable blobs of Winding-River filth stuck to his fur, only to find himself having to duck under the water again to avoid being clouted by a hail of rowing-poles. The galley-saps were rowing more furiously than they'd ever done before.

And a new sound was accompanying their rowing. The merciless thumping of the drum had been replaced by music. The galley-saps were singing as they rowed.

UNTIL WE MEET AGAIN

Spike went down to help Benjamin with the galley-master's heavy key chain and between them they eventually managed to heave it up to the galley-saps' deck. Along with Mops, they each took a key, trying it in lock after lock until they found the one it fitted. Soon every single human galley-sap had been released from their chains.

Benjamin hugged his father, tears of happiness coursing down his face. Duncan Wildfire cried, too. Then, their tears wiped dry, Benjamin told his father how they'd tricked the galley-master into falling overboard and captured the Galley-Royal.

'Well done, Benjamin!' laughed his father. 'I'm so proud of you!'

Benjamin was quick to share the credit. 'Spike and Mops were brilliant. I couldn't have done it without them.'

Duncan Wildfire looked around. 'Where are they?' he asked.

Spike and Mops were nowhere to be seen. Benjamin

had no idea where they might have gone − not, that is, until his father followed his first question with a second, 'So who's steering this Galley-Royal?'

Since being released from their chains, the galley-saps had been singing even louder and rowing even harder. Through the open end of the galley-sap's deck they'd been able to see the wide expanse of the Winding-River stretching ahead. But now…now they could see the walls of the side-quay coming ever closer. Instead of heading away from Bearkingdom-Palace, they were heading straight back towards it again!

With Roger Broadback close behind, Benjamin and his father raced up to the main deck. They found Spike turning the galley-steer, the large many-handled wheel which was used to change the Galley-Royal's direction. Mops was at his shoulder, screeching.

'I said right hand down a bit!'

'What do you think I'm doing!' yelled Spike.

'You're putting your *left* hand down a *lot*, that's what you're doing!'

'I am not! This is my right hand.'

'It's your left hand!' howled Mops. 'Don't you know your left from your right?'

'Do you think I'm stupid?' shouted Spike.

'Yes!' shouted Mops.

'Well I'm not, I'm left-handed. That's the one I always use − which makes it the right one for me!'

Spike and Mops continued arguing, even after Roger

Broadback had taken charge of the galley-steer and with a few deft turns guided them away from danger. Soon the Galley-Royal was back in the deep centre of the Winding-River. There, to the happy sounds of *sing-splash, sing-splash*, Roger Broadback swung the wheel-steer round to set them heading back towards the heart of Lon-denium.

And still Spike and Mops continued arguing. What finally stopped them was Duncan Wildfire asking each of them a question.

To Spike he said, 'What were Bearon Weimar's den and grounds like? Think really hard, Spike. Later on, I'll need you to tell me everything you can remember.'

'Mops,' Duncan Wildfire then said, 'Benjamin tells me you can read.'

'And write,' said Mops with more than a touch of pride.

'Can you read the galley-master's plan-town for me? I need to be shown which parts of Lon-denium and Bear Kingdom Bearon Weimar controls.'

Hearing these questions, Benjamin felt very excited. His father was taking charge. Together they would rescue his mother and become a family again!

Squeezed into the galley-master's alcove, Mops explained to them all what the plan-town said. She pointed with her blue-stained finger as she spoke.

'You see how the plan-town is is divided into four parts by a cross? Well, the whole of Bear Kingdom is divided up in the same way. The middle of the cross is in the centre of Lon-denium, which means that each of the bearons is in charge of part of the town as well.

'There's the End-West which Bearon Herault controls,' said Mops, pointing at the left part of the plan. She then switched her finger to the right as she said, 'and there's the End-East which is looked after by Bearon Drachenloch.'

She paused for a moment, her finger trembling over a small blob marked close to the Winding-River.

'What is it?' asked Benjamin.

'Th-the Howling-Tower,' said Mops with a quavering voice. 'It's in Bearon Drachenloch's region.

'Go on, Mops,' said Duncan Wildfire.

Mops slid her finger down to the section below the blue Winding-River. 'There's the Down-South. That's the part Bearon Sudbury has.' Slowly her sharpened nail traced its way directly upwards, across the river and into the top part of the cross. 'And last of all there's the Up-North. *That's* where Bearon Weimar is in charge.'

Even as she said this, Mops gave a squeak and a gulp. Bending closer to the plan-town she squinted hard at a green oval shape, close to the western edge of Bearon Weimar's part of Lon-denium.

'What is it, Mops?' asked Duncan Wildfire. 'What does it say?'

'It – it says, "Hide-Park"'.

'Hide-Park!' exploded Benjamin. 'Hide-Park is in Bearon Weimar's region! That's perfect! We can go there straight after we rescue my mother!'

Duncan Wildifire laid a gentle hand on his son's shoulder. 'Benjamin, I am going rescue your mother. But not you.'

Benjamin couldn't believe what he'd just heard. His heart felt as though it was packed in ice. Tears welled up in his eyes. 'No!' he cried. 'I'm going with you. I *must* go with you! I don't ever want to leave your side again.'

'You must, my son.' said Duncan Wildfire softly. 'I won't be alone. Roger Broadback and I have talked about this many times. He will come with me.'

Still Benjamin argued. 'But what about me?' he cried.

'You, Mops and Spike must find your way to Hide-Park. You will be safe there. As soon as Roger and I have rescued your mother we will join you. We'll be together then, for all time.'

Hearing this, Benjamin's sorrow flared into anger. 'No!' he raged. 'I won't go with them!' He jabbed an angry finger towards Mops. 'Especially not with her!'

And with that he rushed from the alcove, and up the stairways to the top deck. There he hid himself inside a great coil of rope and cried until he could cry no more.

Benjamin stayed where he was until after dusk.

By then, Roger Broadback had guided the

Galley-Royal expertly into a towering clutch of reeds and weeping willows at the side of the Winding-River. Down below, every galley-sap felt a surge of joy as they released their accursed rowing-pole for the final time. They then lashed a couple of those poles together to produce a makeshift ramp. Almost at once – for they had no possessions to collect – the galley-saps began to run down it eagerly. In twos and threes they vanished into the night, trusting that their future would hold more hope for them than their past.

Only then did Benjamin climb out of his hiding place. He found his father there, waiting for him. At his side were Mops and Spike.

'Benjamin,' said Duncan Wildfire. 'I'm asking you again. Leave me and go to Hide-Park. I will join you there.'

'And what if you don't get there?' pleaded Benjamin. 'I'll be alone!'

Duncan Wildfire smiled. He shook his head. 'With friends such as Spike and Mops you'll never be alone, Benjamin.'

Spike smiled. 'He's right there.' He looked at Mops. 'Or do I mean left?'

'Right,' said Mops, solemnly. She moved forward, reaching for Benjamin's hand. 'Benjamin, we've come so far. It will all work out if we stick together.'

Benajmin backed away angrily. A memory, the same memory he'd recalled when they were studying the plan-town earlier, had bubbled back to the surface. It was a memory he'd tried to erase but simply couldn't.

'Stick together?' he shouted at Mops. 'How can you say that? When I was starving you refused to help me! You call that sticking together?'

'Yes, I do,' said Mops quietly.

She pointed at Spike, a good head taller than Benjamin and a fair bit wider as well. 'Look at him, Benjamin! To stand a chance of beating somebody like him in a fight you had to be absolutely *ravenous*! And if I'd got some food for you – well, you *wouldn't* have been ravenous, would you?'

'And I'd have torn your head off, matey,' nodded Spike. 'Definitely. It would have all been over before you knew it. I'd never have found out who you were and you'd never have found out who I was and – and...' He didn't need to say any more.

'Refusing you was the hardest thing I've ever had to do, Benjamin,' said Mops.

Duncan Wildfire smiled broadly. 'You see, Son, with friends like these I know you won't fail.'

They said their farewells at the bottom of the makeshift ramp. Mops gave Roger Broadback a small piece of parchment onto which she'd copied parts of the plan-town. Benjamin clung to his father for as long as he could. Then, with a final call of, 'Until we meet again!' Duncan Wildfire and Roger Broadback were gone.

It was Mops who broke the long silence they left behind. 'Of course they may not have the slightest problem,' she said. 'It depends on who came out on top in the battle of Bearkingdom-Palace.'

'How come?' asked Spike.

'Simple. If King Antonius and Queen Dearie won, then Chancellor Bruno and those four Bearons will be shut away in a dark dungeon by now – probably minus their heads. Benjamin's father might arrive at Bearon Weimar's den to find it deserted.'

'Then I really hope Bearon Weimar *did* lose,' said Benjamin.

'Oh, *so* do I!' cried Mops. 'It would serve him right for wanting to turn me into a never-move! I can't imagine anything more awful. Not being able to move my arms or my legs...'

'Or your tongue,' grinned Spike.

Benjamin laughed. 'Come on then, which way to Hide-Park?'

'Through these trees to the cart-track on the other side,' said Mops, who'd drawn a little version of the galley-master's plan-town for them to use as well.

Spike squinted at it over her shoulder. 'And then turn right,' he said.

'Left!' snapped Mops.

Benjamin laughed again. His father had spoken wisely. With friends like Mops and Spike, how could he fail?

END OF VOLUME 2

LOOK OUT FOR THE THIRD VOLUME
IN THE BEAR KINGDOM TRILOGY

THE
HUNTING
FOREST

ISBN-10: 1 84616 044 8

ISBN-13: 978 1 84616 044 8

AND DON'T MISS THE FIRST VOLUME

THE
HOWLING
TOWER

ISBN-10: 1 84362 938 0

ISBN-13: 978 1 84362 938 2

Also by **Michael Coleman**

1 84362 183 5   £4.99

'You scared Daniel?'
How many times has Tozer said that to me? Hundreds.

But this time it's different. We're not in school. He hasn't got me in a headlock, with one of his powerful fists wrenching my arm up, asking 'You scared, Weirdo?'

No. We're here, trapped underground together with no way out.

Shortlisted for the *Carnegie Medal, Lancashire Children's Book Award* and *Writers Guild Award*.

'Tense and psychological.' *The Times*

GOING
STRAIGHT

Michael Coleman

1 84362 299 8   £4.99

Luke is a thief who knows that crime *does* pay. Besides, what other way is there for someone like him?

Then he meets Jodi. She might be blind, but she can see where Luke's life is going wrong. And she has a burning ambition that only Luke can help her fulfil...if she can trust him.

So Luke decides to go straight. But when old acquaintances want to use his talents for one last job, can he resist? Or will he end up on the run again?

More Orchard Books

Orchard Books are available from all good bookshops, or can be ordered direct from
the publisher: Orchard Books, PO BOX 29, Douglas IM99 1BQ
Credit card orders please telephone 01624 836000
or fax 01624 837033 or visit our Internet site: www.wattspub.co.uk
or e-mail: bookshop@enterprise.net for details.

To order please quote title, author and ISBN
and your full name and address.
Cheques and postal orders should be made payable to 'Bookpost plc.'
Postage and packing is FREE within the UK
(overseas customers should add £1.00 per book).

Prices and availability are subject to change.